BAD MOON RISING

BAD MOON RISING

ED GORMAN

PEGASUS CRIME
NEW YORK

BAD MOON RISING

Pegasus Crime is an Imprint of
Pegasus Books LLC
80 Broad Street, 5th Floor
New York, NY 10004

Copyright © 2011 by Ed Gorman

First Pegasus Books cloth edition October 2011

Interior design by Maria Fernandez

Library of Congress Cataloging-in-Publication Data is available.

ISBN: 978-1-60598-260-1

10 9 8 7 6 5 4 3 2 1

Printed in the United States of America
Distributed by W. W. Norton & Company

To my friends and saviors
Linda and Randy Siebels

To the websites and e-groups that educate and inspire those of us with the incurable cancer multiple myeloma.

"A hippie is someone who looks like Tarzan, walks like Jane, and smells like Cheetah."

—Ronald Reagan

"Good morning! What we have in mind is breakfast in bed for 400,000."

—Wavy Gravy at Woodstock

"We are not about to send American boys nine or ten thousand miles away from home to do what Asian boys ought to be doing for themselves."

—President Lyndon Johnson

"There's a bad moon on the rise."

—Creedence Clearwater Revival

"Tin soldiers and Nixon coming . . . Four dead in Ohio."

—Neil Young's "Ohio" about Kent State

JESUS CHRIST WAS *NOT* A HIPPIE

In the summer of 1968, the good Reverend Cartwright, last seen setting himself on fire while attempting to burn a huge pile of Beatles records, purchased six billboards around town to make sure that believers and nonbelievers alike got the message that Jesus Christ had not been like hippies during his time on earth.

Three weeks earlier, an eighty-six-year-old woman had written the local newspaper to defend our resident hippies from the slings and arrows of those who hated them. She said that given how the adults had screwed up the world there just might be a chance that these young people had some ideas worth listening to. Further—and you can imagine the bulging, crazed eyes of the good reverend as he read this—further, as a lifelong Christian she was pretty sure that if Jesus Christ walked the earth today he would walk it as a hippie. Not, I assumed, in Birkenstocks, but you get the idea.

So now Reverend Cartwright was on the attack. Seeing the billboard, I realized that it was in fact time for his radio show. Lately I'd been using it as my humor break for the day. For lunch I'd pull into the A&W for a cheeseburger and a Pepsi and sit in my car and listen to his show. It always opened with a tape of his choir—one of the worst I'd ever heard—singing some song about the righteous Lord and how he was going to disembowel you if you didn't do exactly what he told you to do. Then the reverend would come on. He always opened—as he did today—with the same words: "I spoke with God last night and here's what he told me to tell you."

I'd been hearing his show all my life. My father used to listen to it on the days he wasn't working. He'd laugh so hard he couldn't catch his breath at times. I'd be laughing along with him as my mother would peek in and say we shouldn't be wasting our time on a moron like that. But then, she didn't understand our weakness for *The Three Stooges*, either.

Today, as I jammed extra pickles under the top of my bun, the reverend said: "If Jesus Christ was a hippie, as some local infidels are saying, then that would mean that Jesus Christ would sanction what goes on at the commune right on the very edge of our town. A town I have personally sanctified to the Lord. If you will support me with your prayers and your pledges I will see that that commune is closed down and the infidels driven from our midst."

His pitches for money were the dullest part of the show, and since he was obviously headed in that direction I twisted the selection knob looking for some news. I counted three stations playing "Harper Valley P.T.A.," a song critics likened to a three-minute hillbilly version of the novel Peyton Place.

I found a newscast and quickly wished I hadn't. The war the war the war. It had brought down LBJ and had returned to prominence Tricky Dick Nixon.

When I finished eating, I sat back and smoked a cigarette. Right then I felt pretty down, but nothing would compare to how down I would feel less than ten hours later.

PART ONE

1

"I am just way too groovy for this scene, man."

If you were a teenager saying "groovy" you could get away with it. If you were a thirty-four-year-old Buick dealer all gussied up in purple silk bell-bottoms, a red silk shirt, and a gold headband, all you were was one more drunk at a costume party where everybody was dressed up as hippies. Or their idea of hippies, anyway.

"That's you all right, Carleton," I said. "Just way too groovy."

Wendy Bennett gave me a sharp elbow, not happy with the tone of my voice as the six-two Carleton Todd swayed over us, spilling his drink all over his hand. These were her people, not mine. Wendy Bennett came from one of the most prominent families in Black River Falls. Occasionally she wanted to see some of the friends she'd known from her country club days. Some of them I liked and surprised myself by wanting to see again. They were ruining my old theory that all wealthy people were bad. It just isn't that simple, dammit.

"Don't worry about ol' Carleton," Carleton said, his eyes fixing on Wendy's small, elegant breasts. We both wore tie-dyed T-shirts and jeans, our only concession to costume. "I'm used to his insults. I was just in the TV room watchin' the Chicago cops beat up the hippies. Your boyfriend here called me a couple of names in there." He opened his mouth to smile. Drool trickled over his lower lip. "But I called him names right back. If I was a cop I'd club every hippie I saw."

"Carleton, you're a jackass," Wendy said, steering me away before I could say something even nastier.

Don Trumbull's mansion sat on a hill in what had been forest, a bold invention of native stone, floor-to-ceiling windows, and three different verandas. At night the windows could be seen for half a mile. Now, like people in a play of silhouettes, human shapes filled the glass lengths, many of them wobbly with liquor.

"I'm proud of you."

We were on one of the flagstone verandas, the one that loomed over the downslope to the river. Moonlight glittered on the water and stars served as a backdrop to the pines that staggered up the steep incline of the far hills.

Men with Rotarian eyes drifted by, slightly drunk and silly in Nehru jackets. I wondered if they hated costume parties as much as I did. Tonight's fashions were dictated by all the slick magazine spreads about hippies, the problem being that the spreads featured Madison Avenue hippies. Collars so wide and droopy they looked like elephant ears; medallions that would have suited Roman soldiers; and of course fringed leather vests for both men and women.

The hippies I knew really did live back to nature; dungarees for boys and girls alike and nary a Neiman Marcus item among them. The musical *Hair* had become a hit signifying the sexual revolution that people talked about with disdain or envy. There were whispers that the revolution had inspired more than a few people here. Why leave sexual freedom to just the kids? The more we became a bedroom community for Cedar Rapids, the more modern parts of the populace became.

We sat on the edge of the flat stone railing and let the breeze have its way with us. "I always wanted to be in a Disney movie. Did I ever tell you that?"

"No, not that I can remember." The Disney remark signified that she'd reached her limit for the evening. She generally got wistful then and I felt terribly protective of her.

"Not to be Cinderella or anything like that. But to be one of the animals that are always in the forest. They always seem so happy."

I was too much of a gentleman to remind her of Bambi's fate.

"No regrets. No fears. Just grateful to be alive and enjoying nature all day long." Then she giggled. "God, I just remembered what I said to Carleton."

"I'm sure he'll remind you."

"He's really not so bad."

"If you say so."

"C'mon, Sam, it's not that bad, is it? You like some of these people."

"Yeah, I actually do. But most of them aren't here tonight."

"It's summer. A lot of them are on vacation."

She yawned and tilted her perfect head back. When we went to high school together her name was Wendy McKay. Because of the Mc in her name and the Mc in mine we sat together in homeroom where, eventually, she was forced to talk to me. She's admitted now that proximity alone had forced her to converse. We were social unequals. She was from a prominent family whose gene pool had endowed her with shining blonde hair, green eyes, and a body that was frequently imagined when teenage boys decided to seek the shadows for some small-town self-abuse.

She married into the Bennett family believing that her husband loved her. Unfortunately, as she learned all too soon, he'd still been in love with a girl he'd known all his life. After he was killed fighting in Vietnam, it all became moot.

As we had both passed thirty, we didn't try to delude ourselves. She'd gone through a period of sleeping around and drinking too much. She'd ended up spending a lot of money on a shrink in Iowa City. I'd come close to being married three times. We wanted to be married; we even wanted to have a baby or two. But unlike me, Wendy wanted to go slow. So I kept my apartment at Mrs. Goldman's even though I spent most of my nights at her house, shocking numerous guardians of local morality.

"Am I drunk? I can't tell."

"A little."

"Damn. Don't let me do anything stupid."

"Why don't we make a pass through the house once more and then head home?"

I stood up and took her hand. She came up into my arms and we spent several minutes making out like eleventh-graders. I opened one eye and saw over her shoulder the couple who had appeared unheard on the veranda. I smiled at them as I eased out of the embrace. They didn't smile back.

"It doesn't do you any good to watch the tapes of those cops beating up the hippies," Wendy said as we passed through the open French doors and went back inside where three young musicians with long hair were playing guitars and singing Beatles songs. Somebody somewhere was smoking pot. As a lawyer and a private investigator for Judge Whitney, I had the duty to find and arrest this person. I decided to put it off for a few months. "You just get depressed, Sam." She didn't sound as drunk as either of us thought she was.

As we mixed with the throng inside, she said, "Remember, don't watch those tapes again. You get too worked up." Then she hiccupped.

The networks were running tapes of this afternoon over and over again, the ones of Chicago cops clubbing protestors. The protestors weren't exactly innocent. They screamed "Pigs!" constantly; some threw things and a few challenged the cops by running right up to them and jostling them. There were no heroes. But since the cops were sworn to uphold the law it was their burden to control not only the crowd but themselves. Dozens of kids could be seen with blood streaming down their faces. Some lay unmoving on the pavement like the wounded or dead in a war. In the TV room of this mansion several men stood watching the tapes, their hands gripping their drinks the way they would grip grenades. When I'd been in there, about a third of the men were against what the cops were doing. The rest wanted the cops to inflict maximum injury. One man said, "Just kill the bastards and get it over with."

For the next twenty minutes we circulated among the faux hippies. Most of the people we said good-bye to were cordial and even amusing, aware of the irony of middle-aged hippiedom. One man, a school board member I'd disagreed with on a few fiery occasions, even patted me on the shoulder and told me he agreed with me about the Chicago cops. "No excuse for what they're doing. I would've said something in the TV room but I didn't want to get my head taken off." I probably wouldn't be as fiery next time.

For a roomful of people dressed as hippies, most of the conversations sounded pretty square. The men discussed business; the women discussed domestic life and gossiped a bit. While Wendy excused herself to go to the bathroom—still hiccupping—I let a drunken city councilman tell me that he was going to start sending me all his personal legal business because "The big shots want too much money. You have any idea what they charge an hour?" Then, weaving around while he stood in place, he raised his drink, aimed vaguely for his face, and said, the glass a few inches from his lips, "You don't have the greatest reputation, but for the kind of stuff I'll be sendin' you it doesn't matter."

Wendy reappeared and rescued me. Her hiccups were gone. She looked around the largest of the rooms and said, "I wish there were more people from our class here."

"They aren't successful enough to be here. I only got in because you brought me."

"You're like my gigolo." She laughed, but a certain dull glaze remained in her eyes. Where liquor was concerned she was the

7

ultimate cheap date. A couple of drinks and she was at least semi-plastered.

"Let's try the front steps this time," I said.

"Huh?"

I grabbed a cup of coffee for Wendy. We sat on the front steps of the enormous house, enjoying the midwestern night. Trumbull, the man who owned it, was the director of four steel plants. His wife was from here, so they bought this place, turned it into a masterpiece, and lived in it during the warm months. Florida was their home when the cold weather came. The drive that curved around the place was crowded with cars. We'd be long gone by the time most of them left, so we wouldn't have any trouble getting out. But many people well into their cups were going to have some frustrating moments if they all tried to leave at once.

Wendy caught a firefly. She cupped it in her hand and said, "Hello, little fellow."

"How do you know it's a fellow?"

"Take a look."

In the shadow of her hand a golden-green light flickered on and off. "Yep, it's a fella all right."

She laughed and let him go. After her head was on my shoulder she said, "I know these aren't your kind of people, Sam. But remember, your kind of people aren't *my* kind of people, either."

"I thought you liked Kenny."

"I don't mean Kenny. I mean your clients. Some of them are really criminals. I mean bad people."

The front door opened behind us. Our haven had been invaded again. We could have kept on talking but we were self-conscious now. I got up and helped Wendy to her feet.

"Hope we didn't chase you off," a woman's voice said from the shadows.

"No. We were leaving anyway."

When we were out of earshot, Wendy said, "Very nice, Sam. You're really learning social skills."

"You mean instead of saying, 'Look, you sorry bastard, you ruined our whole evening.'?"

"Exactly." She clung to my arm woozily and kissed my cheek. "See, isn't it fun being polite to people you hate?"

"You're crazy."

"Look who's talking."

As we drew closer to my car, I slid my arm around her shoulders. We had our battles, but most of the time there was peace, something I'd never had much of in my past affairs. I'd started to believe what I'd heard a TV pop psychologist say, that some people liked agitation in their relationships. I'd just always assumed that was the way it had to be. But Wendy showed me how wrong I'd been.

Somebody called my name twice. I turned around and shouted back.

"There's a phone call for you, Sam," the female voice said.

I yelled my thanks.

"A client," Wendy said.

"Most likely."

"Poor old Sam."

"Poor old Wendy."

"I don't mind. Right now, relaxing at home sounds better than this anyway."

A woman named Barbara Thomas was waiting for us on the porch. She was another one who'd skimped on costuming herself. A very flattering pair of black bell-bottoms and a white flowing blouse. She'd been in our high school class and had married a lawyer. She was one of those girls who'd ignited many a speculative sexual conversation among boys. She'd always seemed aware of just how stupid we all were.

"Hi, Wendy."

"Hi, Barb. How're your twins?"

"Exhausting but beautiful, thanks. There's a phone in the den, Sam."

They stayed on the porch while I worked my way through the costumed revelers. The den was as big as Wendy's living room and outfitted with enough electronic gear to make me suspect that the owner of the house might be in touch with Mars. He was some kind of short-wave enthusiast. Four different kinds of radios and three different gray steel boxes that made tiny chirping sounds contrasted with the traditional leather furnishings.

I picked up the phone. "Sam McCain."

"Sam. It's Richard Donovan."

"You really needed to call me here, Richard?"

"Look, we've got a real problem out here."

Donovan was the leader of the commune. He brought rules and regs to the otherwise disorganized life out there. When one of his people got in trouble in town—usually being harassed for no reason by one of police chief Cliffie Sykes's hotshots—Donovan was the one who called me.

"And it can't wait until morning?"

"No." Then: "Look, I'm not stoned or anything and I'm telling you, you need to get out here right away."

The tension in his voice told me far more than his words. "You're not telling me anything, Richard."

"Not on the phone. We've had run-ins with the feds before. They may be tapping our phone."

Paranoia was as rampant as VD among the hippies these days. The troubling thing was that some of it was justified.

"I'll be out as soon as I can."

"Thanks, Sam. Sorry I had to bother you."

If the trouble was as serious as it sounded, and if I got involved in it, I would certainly hear from my boss. Though my law practice was finally starting to make reasonable money, my job as private investigator for the judge was still half my income. And Judge Whitney, along with many other people in town (including a couple who kept writing letters about me in the local newspaper), didn't like the idea that I was representing the people at the commune. They wanted the commune and its hirsute folks to move to a different county. Or maybe, if God was smiling that day, out of the state. Judge Whitney didn't believe any of the ridiculous rumors about them—they were satanic and were summoning up the old bastard himself to turn the town into flame and horror being my favorite—but they did violate her notion of propriety, which had come to her down generations of rich snobs who felt that all "little people" were suspicious, period.

I had the feeling that whatever Richard had waiting for me wasn't going to change the minds of either the judge or the two people who kept writing letters about me.

On the porch, Wendy and Barb were smiling. I remembered Wendy telling me that Barb was one friend who hadn't deserted her after her husband died in Vietnam, when she took up the bottle and inhabited a lot of beds that did her no good at all. Both women had warm girly laughs and the sound was sweet on the air, overwhelming the sitar music from inside. Oh, yes, somebody was playing sitar music now. I realize that not liking sitar music marks one as a boor and a likely warmonger and maybe even satanic, but I can't help it. Sitar music should only be played for deaf people.

"Oh, oh," Wendy said.

Barb smiled at me. "Wendy said you'd look a certain way if you were going to go see a client and dump her at home."

"'Dump,'" I said, "is a pretty harsh word."

"How about push me out of the car at a high rate of speed?"

They reverted to their girly laughter, leaning together in that immortal conspiratorial way women have of letting men know that they are hopelessly stupid. I could imagine them at twelve, merrily deflating the ego of every boy who passed by.

"I promise not to go over ninety," I said, lamely continuing the joke.

"Well, I'll have to let you two finish this," Barb said, as if I hadn't spoken. "My husband's in watching TV, and I'd better get in there before he loses all his clients. He made the mistake of telling Walton from the brokerage that if he was ten years younger, he'd probably be a hippie himself. Walton didn't think that was funny. Then they started arguing about the cops beating up all those kids. You know how Walton is. He thought Ike was a Communist. And he was serious."

Wendy slumped against me as soon as Barbara got inside. "Whew. It just caught up with me. One minute I was sober and the next minute I was—"

"—drunk?"

"Again. That's the weird thing. I kind of sobered up but now—"

"Let's get going. I know this curve where I'm going to push you out. It'll be fun."

"Yeah, well, the first thing you'll have to do is help me to the car. I'm really dizzy. All that drinking I used to do. I must be out of practice."

She wasn't kidding. I had to half carry her to the car.

2

A month earlier a gang of bikers had invaded the compound and smashed up the farmhouses and made several of the male hippies strip. For a few people in Black River Falls—anywhere you live there are a few people—it was a tough call. Who was more despicable? Drunken bikers or hippies?

The commune had a history. Shortly after the war two brothers decided to get a GI loan for a large farm they would work together. They built two modest clapboard houses about forty yards apart and proceeded to marry and raise their respective families. They were decorated warriors and popular young men who'd been raised on a farm in a smaller town twenty miles west of Black River Falls. Everything went according to Norman Rockwell for the next nine years, but then, true to many of the stories in the Bible, one brother began to covet the other brother's wife. Well, in fact, he did quite a bit more than covet, and when the cuckold caught his brother and wife making love in the shallow wooded area behind the outbuildings, he became so distraught he ran back to his home, killed their only child (a girl of seven) and then killed himself.

The survivors left the farm, the bank foreclosed, and despite the efforts of a couple of other farmers to buy it and lease it out to starter farmers who couldn't afford the purchase price, the land refused to cooperate. There was a scientific explanation for this, as a state agronomist repeated to anybody who listened, but locals preferred the notion that the land was "cursed" because of what had happened on it.

The hippies came two years ago. Twenty or so of them stayed in the main house, the white one; another fifteen or so stayed in the smaller, yellow house. Some of them worked in town; some of them raised a good share of the food they ate; and a handful, from my observation, were so stoned most of the time that they couldn't do much more than tell you what they'd seen in their last acid vision.

Peace and love, brother. Age of Aquarius. Brotherhood of Man. Every once in a while, stoned on nothing stronger than beer, I'd get caught up in one of the many rock songs that espoused those precepts. But then I'd remember Martin Luther King and Bobby Kennedy, both of whom had died earlier this year, and I'd remind myself of how naïve it all was. There was no peace and love in the slaughter of Vietnam or in the streets of bloody Detroit or Los Angeles.

In some respects I felt sorry for the hippies. I understood in a theoretical way what they were rebelling against. Our country was war-happy and our culture was pure Madison Avenue. What I didn't understand were the ways they'd gone about expressing their distrust of society. I'd look at their babies and wonder what kind of lives the little ones would have. The same for the sanctimony of their language. Without seeming to realize it they were just as doctrinaire as the straight people they put down.

Then there were the drugs, which was how I'd gotten involved with the hippies. Since no other lawyer in town wanted to deal with them, and since the public defender's office had only two attorneys, who worked eighteen-hour days as it was, I decided to help as many as I could. Clifford Sykes, our police chief, was jailing everybody who even looked as if he could spell marijuana (something I doubt Cliffie himself could do).

Marijuana I had no problem with. But I couldn't see the social or spiritual benefits of dropping acid. I'd heard too many stories from the emergency room about young people who never quite recovered from their trips. In March two high schoolers had contrived a suicide plan and had, while acid fractured their minds, locked hands and jumped off Indian Point. They were skewered on the jagged rocks below.

These days chickens, cats, and an arthritic old dog had declared the weedy yard in front of the larger, two-story white farmhouse their private domain. A rusted plow and an old-fashioned refrigerator with the cooling coils on top sat on the edge of the yard, remnants from the farm before it had been deserted by the owners long ago. The enormous garden was in back. They were dutiful about keeping it plentiful. No matter how much pot, acid, and cheap wine filled the night they were up early to work their land. They'd planted corn, carrots, beets, spinach, lettuce, and cabbage. Using a battered wood-fired stove, they also baked bread. That was another surprise. One of them gave me a slice with strawberry jam on it one day, and damned if it didn't taste good.

I snapped off the ignition key and slid out of the new Ford convertible I'd bought after my old Ford ragtop got too expensive to keep fixing up. Or maybe I got it to signal my father, who'd died three years ago, that in my thirties I was finally becoming the man he'd wanted me to be.

Now, as I stood under the glowing span of moon and stars, a song by Crosby, Stills, Nash & Young began streaming from the main house. A breeze fresh as a first kiss made me close my eyes for a moment and ride along with it to long-ago summers when my red Ford ragtop and the lovely Pamela Forrest had been my primary concerns.

When I turned to look at the house I saw Richard Donovan coming down the steps. His father was a colonel in the army, and Richard had inherited his military bearing. Richard even had a uniform of sorts—blue work shirt, brown or black corduroy trousers.

They were always clean. The girls usually wound up doing the laundry for the boys—feminism, the new "ism," had yet to make its mark on this commune—but Richard did his own. I'd seen him hanging his own shirt and a pair of trousers on the clothesline one day. He told me he didn't trust anybody else to keep his stuff the way he wanted it.

In the windows on either side of the front door, faces watched us silently. Whatever had happened out here, everybody knew about it and they were waiting to see how I was going to react when Richard finally told me what was going on.

He was handsome in a severe, gaunt way. There was something of the Old West in the face, pioneer stock I suppose, and now anxiety filled the blue eyes and bulged the hinges of his jaw.

"We have an audience, Richard."

"They're scared."

"Of what?"

"Of what I'm going to show you. They're like little children. If I wasn't here this place wouldn't exist."

Nobody would ever accuse Donovan of being modest. Or having a sense of humor. He was the absolute lord and master of this place as well as the final arbiter. The first few times he paid me to represent him—he didn't seem to have a job so I wondered where the cash came from—he lectured me on how the country was going to be once the government "abdicated" and people like him took over. I didn't like him much, and I suspected the feeling was mutual.

His gaze roamed to the tumbledown, once-red barn downslope from us. In my high school summers I'd detasseled corn, the hottest and hardest work I'd ever done, eight a.m. to seven p.m., in temperatures frequently rising to one hundred. By noon you'd eaten your weight in bugs. At the end of the day, waiting for the bus to take us day laborers back to town, I'd always throw myself on any amount of hay I could find in the cooling barn and go instantly to sleep. This barn, however, looked as though it might collapse on me while I slept.

He nodded in the direction of the lopsided structure and started walking. The ground here was hard and lightly sand-covered. The voices from the watchers grew louder as the music stopped. Some of them were on the porch now. They knew a lot more about what was going on than I did.

The barn was within several yards of the woods and the woods were less than a city block deep. Behind them ran a two-lane gravel county road. High school kids wanting to raise some hell had gotten on the commune property by coming up this way. They waited till late at night when the hippies were asleep and a good share of them stoned as well. They smashed a few windows and spray-painted some swastikas on the houses. Donovan was the only one who confronted them. He jumped on the leader of the kids and broke his nose and arm. Cliffie Sykes had been persuaded to charge only the kids. But the parents of the boy who Donovan had hurt had now sued him in civil court. I'd handle the trial when it came up.

There was no door on the barn. Shadows deeper than night awaited us inside. Donovan stalked right in. I lost him for a few seconds. That's how dark it was. Then suddenly there was light in the form of a dusty kerosene lantern put to life with a stick match he blew out a second too late. He'd burned his fingers and cursed about it.

It was a conventional barn layout with stalls for animals and space for storing equipment. The haymow above us was accessible only by a ladder. The stalls were packed with boxes. This was a storage area. Since a good share of these kids—like some of the other hippies across the land—came from prosperous families, I wondered if they'd brought along some of the goodies from the old days.

The smells ranged from old manure to wood soaked by decades of rain. A few brittle bridles hung from posts; horses had probably been commonplace. As had a leaky ceiling; ruts from tractor tires still gouged the dirt floor in places. Tin signs from the thirties had been nailed to the walls, pop and cigarettes and chewing tobacco and gasoline. This was a time trap; if you stayed here long enough you could probably hear ghost music from that era.

"Nobody here knows anything about this. I want to make that clear."

"I take it somebody's dead."

"Yes." His face was taut with sudden anger. "They'll probably be out here with pitchforks and torches when they find out."

"You're getting ahead of yourself. Calm down."

"Yeah, calm down. All the bullshit we have to put up with just trying to live our lives. You live in a shithole of a town."

He was already getting tiresome. "Show me where the body is." He looked as if he was going to start preaching at me again. "Now."

Donovan walked to a stall that held fewer boxes than the others. "Here." Then: "Superdog kept barking so loud I had to see what was wrong. He brought me over here. At first I thought he was crazy. I mean, who cared about these boxes? But then I took them down. I should trust our dog more."

The boxes were quickly stacked outside the stall. A filthy brown blanket had been thrown over a human body. A small, slender foot with a very white sock protruded from the bottom of the blanket.

I started forward but he stopped me. "I know who she is. She came out here a lot. The whole commune is in real trouble now. I wouldn't be surprised if one of the cops didn't kill her and plant her here to make us look bad."

"That's crazy."

"Well, right now crazy sounds pretty sane to me."

"Who is she?"

"The minute I say her name you'll know how much trouble we're in."

"Humor me. Who the hell is she?"

"It's Vanessa Mainwaring."

"What the hell was Paul Mainwaring's daughter doing out here?"

The laugh was cruel. "A little high-class for pigs like us?"

"Don't give me any more of your overthrow bullshit right now, Donovan, or I might tell you to go to hell and I'll walk away. Don't forget, there isn't another lawyer in town who'll work with you."

I pushed him out of the way and grabbed a rusty rake. Awkward as it was, I managed to ease it under the blanket until I could gently lift it and set it aside. Because I knew her father, I'd seen her a number of times. Now, as she lay on her side, her profile was statue-perfect.

I hunched down. The wounds I could see were concentrated around her heart. There were six of them. Somebody had been very angry with her and had let a knife convey the rage. In books, beautiful dead women always retain some remnant of their beauty. Not so in real life. Heartbreaker that she'd been, now the skin was gray, and the tongue lolling out of the right side of her mouth looked lurid and sickly. Vivid blue eyes stared into eternity; even the dark hair was dusty and flecked with straw.

I looked up at Donovan. "How many people were in this stall to look at her?"

"Just about everybody. Why?"

"You're not stupid, Donovan. You've never heard of a crime scene? The cops'll look for all kinds of evidence. People tramping around in here'll just make it tougher for them."

"Cliffie's a moron. He won't look for any evidence at all."

I pushed against my thighs to stand up and face him. "Cliffie's daddy hired a so-called police commander to do all the serious work. The old man got tired of everybody bitching about his son. The police commander's name is Mike Potter and he was a detective in Kansas City for six years before he had a heart attack and decided to look for a nice little nook to spend the rest of his career. He's good. And the first person he'll want to talk to is you. And one of the first questions he's going to ask is how many people tramped around in the barn after you found her body."

"You mean I was supposed to stop them?"

He wanted to argue. His question had been an accusation. "Who put the blanket on her?"

"I did."

"What time did your dog start barking?"

19

"Maybe an hour and a half ago. And listen—I'm not some zombie, man. I'm sorry she's dead, if that's what you're worried about. But I also kinda run this place, you know. I've got to worry about everybody else, too."

"Who did she know out here?"

"Everybody. She tried hard to fit in but most of the people didn't like her."

"Why not?"

He took the time to slide a package of Pall Malls out of his shirt pocket. He was stalling.

"Why didn't they like her?"

"Because of Neil, Neil Cameron."

I'd had to represent Cameron a few times. He had a temper. When townspeople hassled him, he hassled back. "What about Neil?"

"She kind of jacked him around."

"He went out with her?"

This time he got a full one-act play out of lighting his cigarette with a stick match. "Some people said he was obsessed with her. When she broke up with him he just kind of . . ."

"Kind of what?"

He shrugged lean shoulders. "You know what it's like when you're dumped. You get crazy for a while."

"Was he still crazy these days?"

He was good at evasion. "I don't know. You'd have to ask him."

"Where do I find Cameron now?"

"I'm not sure. His sister would know."

"Sarah Powers?"

"Oh, that's right. You handled a couple of cases for her, too."

Neil and Sarah had different last names because their parents were killed before the kids were even ten, and different sets of aunts and uncles raised them.

"Sarah doesn't like you very much."

"Then we're even. I don't like Sarah very much, either."

She was one of the troublemakers out here. She'd been ticketed for parking the van in a No Parking zone and then had screamed at the cop while he was making out her summons. Then she got in another screaming match with a check-out woman at one of the supermarkets, accusing the woman of overcharging her because she was a hippie. Two weeks ago she was in a record store telling all the customers that they should steal anything they wanted, that the filthy capitalists were ripping off the country and getting away with it. The owner of the store called me and said if I didn't remove her in five minutes—she had threatened to punch him if he touched her—he'd call the police. Fortunately, I'd been in my office and got there in time. The owner was a twenty-eight-year-old who fancied himself to be very counterculture. I wondered how he was feeling about things now that he'd heard Sarah's everything-for-free rap.

"Let me see the soles of your sandals."

"Why?"

"I want to check footprints. I need to eliminate yours and mine."

He wore tire-tread sandals, easy to identify. I checked my own, then began dragging the lantern low over the immediate area. There were numerous fresh imprints. "You said 'just about everybody' was in here looking. How many people would that be?"

"Well, not everybody's here tonight. I suppose fifteen or twenty."

"You should've sold tickets."

"Hey man, you'd be interested, too, a dead girl in your barn. It's natural to be curious."

"Let's go find Sarah."

He put his fingers against my chest as if he didn't want me to move. He shook his head as if I'd said something he didn't agree with. "Look, I might as well tell you."

I shoved him away. "Tell me what?"

"About Neil." He sighed. "And Vanessa. They—she came out here the other night and he started screaming at her. We were all afraid he'd hurt her or something. Finally Sarah broke it up. She didn't want to see Neil hurt Vanessa. She and Van were good friends."

"So you think Neil killed her?"

"I didn't say that."

"Yes, you did." I wondered why it had come so easily from him. He'd been protective of everybody in the commune and then he set Neil Cameron up with a motive and a possible foreshadowing of the murder.

"I feel like hell telling you about Neil."

I almost smiled. He was a terrible actor. "Yeah, I can tell."

His eyes narrowed in the dusty gold of lantern light. He was probably trying to figure out if there was any sarcasm in my response.

I walked to the rear of the barn. The doors hung askew and there was a wide gap separating them. An average-sized person could walk between them with no problem. I went out and stood in the back. At this point the woods were close. A person who'd climbed up the hill from the road below wouldn't have had any trouble sneaking into the barn without being seen.

I went back inside.

"Let's go find Sarah."

I was glad to leave the barn, to enjoy the healing effects of the stars and the breezes of the night. I could see that at least six or seven people stood on the porch watching us. The music was off. Pot odor got stronger the closer we got to them. One of them was Sarah Powers, hands on hips, glaring at me. Before we even got there she snapped, "What's he doing here, Richard?"

"He's going to help us."

"You're such a child, Richard. He's here to get us in trouble and for no other reason." She had a tomboy rage that made her as formidable as a boy, forty pounds overweight, an unattractive round face and dark eyes that seemed to have only two expressions: contempt and rage. She tried to hide her own misery by taking it out on others.

"I want him off our land," she said as we walked up to her.

"'Fraid you can't do that, Sarah. I'm an investigator for Judge Whitney. That gives me the right to arrest people, and if you try obstructing justice, I'll arrest you."

"Thanks for inviting him here, Richard. You did exactly the wrong thing as usual."

"I need to talk to your brother."

"He isn't here."

"Where is he?"

"I wouldn't know."

"He could be in serious trouble, Sarah. Believe it or not, I'm trying to help him."

"I'm the only one who can help him. If he did what I tell him, he'd never get in trouble."

"The police'll be looking for him as soon as they hear about this."

"A lot of people had reason to kill her. Don't try to shit me, McCain."

"A lot of people may have had reason to kill her, but not a lot of people had the opportunity to kill her in your barn. That's the first thing the police'll jump on."

"C'mon, Sarah, help him."

"All you care about is this stupid commune, Richard. You don't care about Neil."

"He's my friend, Sarah. You're forgetting that."

"If he's your friend, what's McCain doing here?"

As she spoke, and for the third time, I saw her eyes glance at the small rusted Airstream west of the house. If he hadn't run away, that might be the place he'd choose to gather himself and plan what he was going to do next.

"Donovan, I want you to come with me. I want to check out the trailer."

"No!" There was pain rather than anger in her voice. She was protecting her brother.

"C'mon, Donovan."

She grabbed my arm. "You can't do this, McCain. He didn't kill her."

"Then he needs to tell the police that." I removed her hand from my arm. I nodded to Donovan and we started walking to the trailer.

The group on the porch was still watching us. By now sweat was streaming down my chest and back. Despite our words I felt sorry for Sarah. She was right. Cliffie and the local paper would convict Cameron without a trial. The people who hated the commune would use the murder as a pretext for getting rid of it entirely.

The trailer had been left here by the farmer and his wife who'd tried leasing it the second time. They couldn't afford to fix up either of the houses to live in so they'd bought this old tin trailer. They'd left it behind with their dreams.

As we walked I said, "When we get done here, I want you to go to your house and call the police. Tell the woman on duty there what happened and tell her we need the chief to come out here with an ambulance. I'm going to guard the barn so nobody else gets in there."

I could hear her coming behind me. The ground was covered with rocks and pieces of wood, probably blown here in one of the many tornadoes the area had endured over the years. She was running. I shifted to the left, in case she'd already launched herself at me. But all she wanted, breathless, was to talk.

"He's in there, McCain. In the trailer, I mean."

"All right."

"But he's got a gun and I don't want him to do anything crazy. The mood he's in—he might try to kill himself."

I put my hand on her shoulder. "Look, Sarah, I'm not trying to be a hard-ass here. I just want Neil to talk to the police. We both know they're going to say he did it. If I was a cop I'd be inclined to say that, too. They had an argument. Neil couldn't deal with losing her. She was found in the barn. But the only alternative right now is that he runs away and if he does that he's in real trouble. He might be some-place where a trigger-happy cop spots him and kills him. Fugitive on the run. Happens all the time, Sarah."

Grief replaced anger. I took my hand away. I saw the youngster in her. Hers hadn't been a happy life, not looking the way she did. School kids could hurt you worse than bullets, with wounds that never healed.

"You don't give a damn about him."

"I'd like to see him clear himself if he can."

"You already think he's guilty and he isn't." Tears gleamed in her eyes.

"Good. That's what I want to hear him tell me. Now let's you and I go talk to him."

She glanced back at the people on the porch as if for reassurance. A shadowy male shouted, "Don't trust him, Sarah."

"He's wrong, Sarah. Right now Neil needs me more than ever. I'm the only legal friend he's got."

Donovan spoke quietly. "He's right, Sarah. You need to listen to him."

Grief became anger. "You want him to be guilty, Richard."

I had no idea what she was hinting at. "Let's find him, Sarah. Right away, before things get any worse."

"How could they get any worse?"

"By not calling the police as soon as possible. If there's a long lag between the time I saw the body and calling them, it'll look very bad for everybody. Now c'mon."

"You better be telling me the truth about helping Neil."

"I am."

I turned toward the trailer. After half a minute she joined me and we set off. My shirt and trousers had sweated to me like a second skin. The alcohol kick from the party was long gone. The ground here was rough and rocky. I almost stumbled twice.

We were now ten yards away.

"I'll go ahead and talk to him. He's *my* brother."

"All right."

"You stay back here until I tell you to come in."

She was in a hurry now. I saw a silhouette of him, backlit by the sudden lantern light inside, watching her rush to him. Then the door squeaked open and she disappeared into the dim doorway.

I smoked. I smoked three cigarettes in the next twenty minutes. I could hear their voices but not their words. Sometimes there was the sharp noise of anger, sometimes there were sobs. There were even lengthy silences. I thought of all the things they were probably saying to each other. From what I knew of him, Neil probably wasn't about to turn himself in. But she would be pleading. I'd raised the prospect of him being killed by some overeager cop. I had the feeling that these were the words that had scared her into helping me.

A stray brown mutt came up and looked me over with big sweet eyes. Apparently she didn't like what she saw. She trundled away. I looked back at the houses. They were all in the front yard now, waiting to see what would happen. "In a White Room" was being played, but at a much lower volume than the earlier records. The heat and plain exhaustion were making standing difficult. I'd had a long day and now I was facing an even longer night.

The trailer swayed. Heavy footsteps. The door swung open. Sarah appeared. She half shouted: "Neil says you can come to the door and talk to him but you can't go inside."

"He's giving the orders now?"

"He's scared. You can't understand that?"

"He'll have to come out eventually."

"That's your problem. Right now you just get to stand in the doorway, all right?"

I had my .45. I'd talk to him in the doorway and then I'd go inside and get him. Apparently desperation had confused her. She assumed that I'd really put up with this and not make my move.

"All right, Sarah."

She stepped away from the trailer. She had her hands on her hips as I walked toward her. When I got closer she said, "Don't hassle him. He doesn't need to be hassled."

"Right."

"And keep your sarcasm to yourself. He's my brother." I wondered how many times tonight she was going to remind me of that.

I approached the door and she stepped aside.

"Remember what you agreed to."

"I remember."

Smells coming from the open trailer door almost gagged me. Several decades of filth combined to become a weapon. I started to stick my head inside but she got me before I was able to finish the move.

At the time I had no idea what she hit me with. Nor did I have time to think about it. My skull felt as if it had been cleaved in half. A headache that seemed to instantly shut down my entire body left me unable to defend myself when she yanked me backward and struck me with even more force a second time. I have no idea what happened next.

3

In high school Alan Nevins was inevitably called "Four Eyes" because of his thick glasses. We were friends because we read science fiction. I doubled up on Gold Medal novels of course, but since all the books and magazines we wanted could be found at the same drugstore— specialists in cherry Cokes—we always ran into each other. He was a relentless smart-ass. He was also now my doctor. He'd taken care, good care, of my father in his last two years. He was Wendy's doctor as well. I was sitting on a bed in a large room filled with three gurneys and cabinets on every wall filled with various drugs and implements. Alan was sewing nine stitches into the back of my head and obviously enjoying the hell out of me wincing.

"He's too cute to die, doctor. Is he going to make it?" Wendy said.

"Yes, he is pretty cute, now that you mention it. But it's going to be touch and go," the good doctor said as he finished his work.

"Very funny, you two."

I hadn't planned on coming back to the hospital in which my father died for a long time. Years, hopefully. But here I was, as much confused as hurt. I had a ghost memory of being put in the flower power van out at the commune and taken here. The memory extended to clutching a phone in my hand and telling Mike Potter about the Mainwaring girl and where he could find her.

"Do you think an injury like this could change his personality, doctor?"

"I'm afraid not. He'd have to be hit on the head a lot harder than he was tonight."

"I think I could arrange that."

I couldn't help it. I laughed, and when I laughed my skull cracked right down the middle again. I pressed my hands to my temples, as if I could crush the pain.

"Oh, I'm sorry, Sam," Wendy said, taking my hand. "You should've seen your face just then. No more jokes."

Then there were three of them. Mike Potter, in his police tans, had joined them. He was a short, wide, fierce-looking man who needed to shave three times a day. The mild, reasonable voice emanating from that baleful face always surprised people and put them at their ease, sometimes at their peril.

"How you doing, Sam?"

"I guess Doc thinks I'll live."

"I know a lot of people who won't want to hear that."

"Another comedian."

He smiled. Of all Cliffie's gendarmes, Potter was the most streetable one. His years as a Kansas City homicide detective had given him a professional manner not usually seen on the streets of Black River Falls. He looked at Wendy and Alan. "I'd like five minutes alone with Sam here if you wouldn't mind."

"No problem," Alan said.

"If you're going to beat him, could we stay and watch?"

"I won't beat him right away, Wendy. But when you hear him start screaming, feel free to come back and watch."

"This is like comedy night on *Ed Sullivan*," I said.

Wendy very carefully placed a tiny kiss on my forehead and then disappeared with Alan. Potter went over to a coffeepot I hadn't noticed and poured himself a cup. He waggled an empty one at me. I started to shake my head but it hurt too much so I just said "No."

He pulled up a chair next to my bed and sat down. His military-tan shirt was sweated through in many places. "I think those hippies set a record for contaminating a crime scene in that stall where the girl was."

"You noticed that, huh?"

"They really that stupid?"

"Not stupid. Just—they were curious is all."

He set his coffee cup on the floor, then yanked a package of Viceroys from his shirt pocket. I did the same with my own brand. His Zippo got both of us smoking.

"In case you're interested, the Powers girl had a thick steel rod stuffed into the back of her jeans. That's what she hit you with. She's a tough little cookie. Sort of mannish."

"I take it her brother escaped."

"That's what hitting you was all about. Give him time to get away."

"And nobody at the commune went after him?"

"They're not what you call upstanding citizens."

Most times I would have defended them. Right now I wasn't feeling gracious.

"You know this Neil Cameron?"

"Yeah. I defended him a few times in court."

"The boys at the station tell me he's a real bastard."

"He can be."

"Enough of a bastard to kill Vanessa Mainwaring?"

"I can't say."

"Can't or won't? He's your client."

"Can't. I haven't been asked to defend him in this case, anyway. And besides, I don't think you've got enough to arrest him. All you can do is bring him in for questioning."

"The chief thinks we've got our man."

"The chief always thinks that."

"He wants to see you, by the way. Tomorrow morning at your convenience. Which means as early as possible." He picked up his coffee. It was cooler now and he drank it down. He got up and carried the cup over to the sink. He came back and said, "You and Paul Mainwaring are friends, I'm told."

"Not really friends, friendly I guess you'd say. We agree on a lot of things politically and so we wind up at meetings sitting together and talking."

"Gee, the chief says you two are Communists."

"Does he still carry that photo of Joe McCarthy in his billfold?"

Potter smiled. "I stay away from politics. I hate them all. Anyway, you go see the chief first thing tomorrow, all right?"

"Sure."

"Sarah Powers is in our jail now and she'll stay there until somebody bails her out. I doubt the hippies can raise the money but maybe they'll surprise us." He went to the door and said, "Glad you weren't hurt, Sam. But those kids were bound to get in trouble. I suppose a lot of people have told you that."

"Just a couple thousand." To his back, I said, "Thanks, Mike."

He opened the door and stood aside as Wendy and Alan came back in. She watched him out and then closed the door. "He's so nice."

"He's so nice as long as he thinks you haven't done anything wrong. Then he's not so nice at all."

They came over to my bed.

With his acne gone and his style of glasses more fashionable, Alan had grown well into his medical whites. He had a red Corvette and a number of girlfriends. The only thing he lacked was hair. Two years from a bald pate for sure. He put his hand on my shoulder. "You're going to have your headache for at least twenty-four hours, maybe longer. I've given you some pills that will help. I'd say right now let's have Wendy take you home and make you comfortable."

"You did such a great job on Sam, Alan."

"I inflicted all the pain I could on him, Wendy. I did the best I could."

31

Wendy was of course delighted. She giggled.

"He's all yours, Wendy. Good luck. Sam, I gave her instructions on what to watch for and how to take care of you. She's got my card. I wrote my home number on the back of it. If anything changes, call me. Now I've got some really sick patients to see."

Just as the door closed, Wendy said, "I've never been in charge of anybody before. This'll be fun. I'll be back in a minute. While I'm gone, don't do anything dumb, Sam."

"Such as?" ·

"Such as trying to walk. Alan told me you'd be unsteady on your feet."

"Yes, boss."

Her lovely red lips bloomed into a smile. "I like the sound of that."

While she was gone I eased myself off the examination table and tested my legs. Shaky, but not as bad as Alan predicted. I walked over to the sink. I moved slowly, carefully. There was a moment when my left leg lurched wildly. I stood absolutely still, waiting for the shock of the lurch to recede. Then I started walking again, much more slowly this time.

I made it to the sink and back before Wendy returned.

"Good boy," she said. "I'm sure you were walking around while I was gone but I appreciate you pretending you didn't." She put her hand on my shoulder. "Come on, let's get out of here."

I didn't argue.

At Wendy's I lay on the couch watching a rerun of I Love Lucy while Wendy worked in the kitchen. My impression was that I dozed off for a few minutes. But when I woke up to the aromas of good food, Wendy informed me that I'd been out for nearly forty-five minutes and that she hadn't started breakfast until she heard me stirring.

"I thought you might like this. Scrambled eggs, French toast, bacon, orange juice."

"God, thank you, I'm starved."

"Sit up then, we'll go out to the breakfast nook. I wanted to entice you with this food in case you tried to tell me you weren't hungry."

"Thank you very much, Wendy."

"How's your head?" she asked as she helped me up off the couch.

"Tolerable."

"How about the stitches?"

"Sting a little."

"I'll run some warm water on a washrag and hold it against your wound while you eat." She kissed me on the cheek. "So eat."

I ate. A window in her breakfast nook allowed me to glance outside at a backyard filled with the green, green grass and the blue and red and yellow of various birds that were almost, but not quite, as beautiful as those in Disney animation. Wendy held the washrag against the back of my head for nearly fifteen minutes. She did this while sitting in a chair and drinking coffee and smoking Winstons. "Lady Madonna" played low on the radio.

"Do you remember me helping you to bed?"

"Vaguely. I was exhausted. And maybe I just didn't want to think about everything that had happened so I blacked out."

"Survival tactic."

"That sounds like something your shrink would say."

"He talks like that."

"You sure he's not trying to get you into the sack?"

"That was the last one. That's why I got this new one. And this new one looks very tame. He wears Hush Puppies. I'm pretty sure if you wear Hush Puppies you're faithful to your wife."

I hate laughing with my mouth full.

Then she said: "It's in the paper. They make you sound like a hero. How you suspected there was something wrong about that trailer and how you went to arrest Cameron and how his sister knocked you out."

There was a reason for the favorable treatment. A distant cousin of mine was now the editor. If Cliffie could rely on kin, why shouldn't I? But Wendy was only repeating what my mother, my friend and landlady Mrs. Goldman, and Kenny had told me earlier this morning when they'd called to see how I was doing.

"Well, we'll see how it plays with the people. Cliffie will say I got beaten up by a girl."

"Did I ever tell you that Cliffie groped me once?"

I had to speak around a large bite of French toast. "Cliffie did?"

"One of those Christmas dances for charity. Several years ago. Cliffie'd had plenty of eggnog. He grabbed me and dragged me to the dance floor. I swear that guy has six hands. Just when I was brushing his hand off my bottom he started dry-humping me. He even started kissing my neck. I was worn out after one dance. And I knew he remembered because every time he'd see me afterward he'd look away. This went on for a long time. Now he's back to ogling me. So don't worry about what Cliffie thinks. He's an idiot."

The kitchen phone was a bright yellow. It was affixed to the wall next to the counter space in the kitchen and its ring complemented the color. It trilled yellow. Honest.

I enjoyed watching her walk to the phone in her red shorts and loose white blouse. A comely woman. When we were apart I could actually feel her sleep warmth. I considered that a very good sign.

"Hello." Then: "He's right here."

She held the phone out to me and when I took it she was nice enough to lean into me and kiss me on the cheek again.

"Are you all right? I was so scared reading about you. I've said a lot of prayers already. Oh—sorry. Good morning, Mr. C. I should have said that first I guess."

My secretary, Jamie, has come a long way. She still can't type but at least she catches about half her mistakes and retypes them over Wite-Out. The problem here being that she's a bit sloppy with the white stuff so that it tends to run down the page and smear some of the words below. But the fault is mine. I was forced to take her in trade from her father who couldn't pay the bill he owed me for representing him in court. She's cute and sexy and as good-hearted as Bambi. Despite my attempts to explain why Turk, the lazy, shallow, and self-absorbed love of her life, was bad for her, she went back to him after a long break-up Wendy and I had helped along. Turk had apparently interpreted their wedding vows to include his right to hit his wife, which he'd done on at least one occasion.

"Good morning, Jamie."

"I really like Wendy, Mr. C. You two should get hitched."

The "Mr. C" owes to the fact that the people on Perry Como's TV show called him "Mr. C." I know—my name doesn't begin with C. But as Jamie explained, "There's a C in the second and third letters."

"We're working on that, Jamie. What's going on?"

"The police station called and they said that Sarah Powers wants you for her attorney."

Days that began with surprises were not my favorite. Somehow the surprises were always bad. "All right. I'll stop there before I come in this morning."

"Oops. There's the other line, Mr. C."

I finished my eggs and a fresh cup of coffee while telling Wendy about Sarah Powers.

"Be careful she doesn't still have that steel rod. You sure you want to help her?"

"No."

"Then why do it?"

"Because there's nobody else who'll sign on. And she definitely needs help."

"You have a lot of other things to do."

"I just hate to see her in jail. She's sort of a sad case. In her mind she was just trying to help her brother."

"Why is she a sad case?"

"The ugly girl. The fat girl. The boyish girl. Easy to imagine how the other kids treated her growing up. She and Cameron lost their parents when they were still kids. She was defending the only real friend she's ever had."

"I hate to remind you, Sam, but you're still wincing from your headache because of her."

"Maybe I'm doing it just to piss off Reverend Cartwright."

She poked me on the shoulder. "Now there's a reason I can understand, Sam."

4

"Hippies," Cliffie Sykes said. "I had my way we'd deport their asses."

"Sounds reasonable to me."

The police station was relatively new, thanks to a matching grant from Sykes Foundation. Old man Sykes even sprang for some new Western-style uniforms. Now all the officers dressed like Cliffie, military tans and campaign hats. He had the usual state-celeb political black-and-whites framed on the wall along with a melancholy painting of Jesus.

Behind him, the centerpiece of the office—ruling over all four dark green filing cabinets, the desk, the three-button phone, and the family portrait—was an outsized framed photo of John Wayne all dressed up as a marine in his laughable propaganda movie *The Green Berets*. I preferred looking at the family portrait. Cliffie's youngest daughter suffered from spina bifida. When you saw how gentle and loving Cliffie was with her, you couldn't quite hate him for the bumbling, bigoted fool he was. You could dislike him but not hate him, though I was in a pissy enough mood to give him grief. While I didn't have a steady headache, I did have attacks of sharp pain that forced me to close my eyes and grit my teeth. "You like 'em, don't you? You and friend Kenny, you guys were beatniks and now you're hippies." I was here to see Sarah Powers, but as Potter had told me last night, I needed to see Cliffie first—the mandatory endurance contest I always had to survive.

"Kenny was a so-called beatnik when we were juniors in high school. I never was. And neither of us are hippies. I mean, if you want to get your facts straight for once."

"Yeah, well, he still writes dirty books."

"He writes other things, too." I was counting on Cliffie's lack of interest in everything literary. He didn't ask me to tell him exactly what those "other things" were. In addition to paperbacks such as *Satan's Love Slaves* and *Lesbo Lodge*, Kenny had now started writing for men's adventure magazines. You know the ones I mean. The guys never have shirts on and they're usually under attack by Nazis or killer dogs. Well, for that matter, the women don't have shirts on, either, and they're frequently attacked by Nazis and killer dogs. But the women don't have scars all over their mostly naked bodies and they aren't holding machine guns. "Nazi Terror Orgies" was one of Kenny's latest. This was not to be confused with "Nazi Lust Prisons." Kenny had a very good novel in him somewhere; he still wrote seriously good short stories for himself. I had faith in him; his wife, Sue, had faith in him. All we had to do was convince Kenny to have some faith in himself.

"I had my way, we'd put all those pornographers in jail. And that goes for the Smothers Brothers."

Why correct him? The Smothers Brothers' politics offended him— offended more than half the nation—so their TV show had become a focal point for all the people who thought that the Vietnam War was just a dandy idea.

But this was just sparring and we both knew it. The main bout would start with something else, something he just couldn't wait to spring on me.

"I stopped by the Blue Moon Tap and told 'em what happened to you."

"Had a good laugh, I'll bet."

"Couple of 'em were laughin' so hard I thought they'd puke."

"Well, thanks for telling me, Chief."

"One guy had beer runnin' out of his nose he was laughin' so hard."

"I'll bet that was you, wasn't it?"

He glared at me. I'd found him out. Glare became glower and he said: "So a girl knocks out Sam McCain and the prisoner escapes."

He was saying that real men don't get knocked out by women. "I guess you could tell it that way if you wanted to."

"Oh, I want to, McCain. I really want to. All the crap I've had to take from you over the years. You and that g.d. judge of yours. All the b.s. about how you solved my cases before I did. And you with your law degree and the private investigator's license your judge made sure you got so you could snoop around. You damn right that's the way I want to tell it. And that's the way just about everybody in this town's gonna tell it. Hotshot Sam McCain tries to collar a killer and gets knocked out by a girl so the killer gets away. That'll look real nice in the state paper."

Before he'd mentioned the state paper his words hadn't had their desired effect on me. I knew that the people in Black River Falls who didn't like me (and the number seemed to grow every year) would have their fun. I'd be embarrassed and sometimes I'd get mad and sometimes maybe I wouldn't want to leave my office. But Wendy would help me through it and if I got lucky enough to look good on a few more cases, the story about Sarah smacking me with a steel rod would fade in time. Never disappear, nothing ever does; but fade. But now I imagined what the story would look like under a bold headline in the state paper. They had a photo of me a few years back following a trial I'd won. The trouble was I'd just gotten done tripping on a step in front of the county courthouse so my expression was that of shock and dismay when the photographer snapped his pic. Hapless was what I looked like—hapless.

Cliffie was taking such pleasure in my embarrassment I couldn't help myself. If he could be petty so could I. I realize that the thought of Sam McCain being petty—unthinkable. But—

I nodded to his framed melodramatic photo of big John Wayne in his Green Beret getup. "You do know John Wayne was a draft dodger, don't you?"

"What the hell're you talkin' about? Some lefty crap you thought up?"

"Not crap, Chief. Facts. It's in several books. He decided against serving because he was afraid he wouldn't have a career when he came back—even though most other stars enlisted. So they trumped up some health problem and the draft board went along with it because they're part of Hollywood, too. So now you have big brave Duke calling war protestors draft dodgers. Kind of a hypocrite, wouldn't you say?"

"Just because it's in a book doesn't mean it's true."

"No, but people who knew him at the time agreed that it was true."

"Lefty crap."

"Which is the reason you always give for sending your officers out to harass the people who live on that farm. Because they're all 'lefties.' I thought we had an agreement you were going to lay off."

"I'll lay off when they start wearin' shoes and having some respect for this country and cuttin' their hair so you can tell the boys from the girls."

"Yeah, that's a real problem, all right. I get confused all the time."

"You think it's funny. But it sure as hell isn't. A lot of people want to run 'em out on a rail. Reverend Cartwright says he can't sleep at night thinkin' of all the fornicatin' that's goin' on out there."

I couldn't help myself. I smiled.

"What's so funny?"

"Just thinking of Reverend Cartwright and all that fornicating. Must be driving him crazy." I stood up. "I take it we're through here."

"I don't believe a word you said about John Wayne."

"Up to you, Chief. But it's true. He was a draft dodger."

He waved me off. Then grinned. "You be careful walkin' around town, McCain. There might be a teenage girl lookin' for a fight. And you know how mean they can be."

There wasn't much point getting mad. I was going to be hearing a lot more of it in the days to come.

5

Harry Renwick, a guy my father had bowled with, led me past several prisoners. Two of them were former clients of mine. One waved and one smirked. The smirker still owed me money.

I'd used the two interrogation rooms many times. Harry opened the first door. I went in and sat down at a bare table with four chairs around it. I didn't need to light up. There was about a carton of smoke still on the air from the last few interrogations.

"How's your mom doing, Sam?"

"Still trying to believe Dad's really gone."

He smiled. "Those World War Two guys, they always told us we had it easy in Korea."

It seemed more and more that the American Dream had turned into a war for every generation.

"Yeah, my dad could really get going sometimes."

"He was a great guy, Sam. One of my best friends. And he sure was proud of you." I'd wondered what was wrong with me after my father passed on. I never cried. I knew in the abstract I wanted to but somehow the tears never came. Now sometimes at odd moments I just wanted to let go. This was one of those moments, sitting here in an interrogation room where people were dragged to confess the terrible things they'd done—I just wanted to put my head down and wail for the father I loved so much. And who I'd never see again.

A knock on the half-opened door. Sarah Powers stood there in the two-piece maroon jail uniform. She looked heavy, pasty, and angry. The only fashion accessory she'd been allowed were the handcuffs. A police matron nudged her inside.

Harry pulled a chair back for her. She sat down. Only when she was seated for a time did I see how fatigue had drawn crevices in her face.

The matron, a scrawny Irish woman, said, "I'll be right outside."

"You tell your mom I said hi."

"I sure will, Harry. Nice to see you." Then, whispering, I said: "This room bugged?"

Harry shook his head. "Not this one. The one down the hall."

After he was gone, Sarah said, "It was either you or a public defender. I didn't have any choice."

"You trying to flatter me?"

"Oh, go to hell, McCain."

"We're off to a good start."

Silence.

"How're you doing in here?"

Silence.

"You asked for me, remember? You keep this up, I'm going to walk out the door. You understand me?"

She raised her cuffed hands to her face and sighed. After she put her hands on the table again, she said, "There's a woman in my cell who left her baby in her car for three hours while she was in some dive seeing her boyfriend while her husband was home sleeping off a hangover. Thank God a cop came along and found the little baby. The woman was telling me that she shouldn't be in here. That she's actually a good mother. This is the second time she's done this. Then there are the two prostitutes. And the woman who embezzled money from the trucking company where she worked. Not exactly the kind of people I'm used to."

I took out my cigarettes and placed them on the table. I sat close enough to give her drags.

She didn't thank me but her tone changed. It was as if she was suddenly too tired to argue. "Neil wasn't like this before he went to Nam. He was just a nice, normal kid. But when he came back— They actually had to put him in a mental hospital for three months."

"Tell me how he changed."

"He'd always been kind of quiet. Got average grades. Never got in trouble. Wasn't a big reader but he loved going to movies. He went to junior college—this was in Des Plaines where we grew up—and he really liked it. He started getting interested in books for the first time. But then he got his draft notice. They didn't think junior college was good enough for a deferment so they shipped him off. He didn't write much, and when he did, he didn't really tell me anything. He'd talk about the food and the local customs but nothing about how he felt or anything. In his letters he didn't sound the same anymore. I always figured he'd tell me everything when he got back."

"Did he?"

"No. But a kid he served with told me about something that happened to Neil over there. They were approaching this sort of hamlet—there were five of them—and there was firing from two of the huts. While four of them worked on the two huts, Neil swung around and checked out the other three. He heard noise in one of them and opened fire. When he looked in to see who'd been in there he found two little girls. They'd been huddled in the corner. His bullets had torn them apart. He said Neil was never the same after that. When they'd go into Saigon all Neil wanted to do was get drunk and start fights. My brother Neil, fighting? He might have been in a few shoving matches on the playground but that was the extent of it. And now he was always picking on bigger and tougher guys who were sure to hurt him pretty bad. You don't have to be a psych major to know that he wanted somebody to punish him, do you?"

Her shoulders slumped and she exhaled long and hard. Not even hatred can exhaust you the way love can. "He was that way when he got back home, too. He had nightmares that woke up the whole house. My biggest fear was that he was going to kill himself. And in a way he tried to. All the fights and two drunk driving arrests and confrontations with half the people he ran into. I thought when he met this girl Jenny he might come out of it at least a little ways. He cleaned himself up physically and cut way back on the alcohol. He was always decent to me. I think I was the only person he'd ever really trusted.

"It went well for three or four months, with Jenny I mean. One night he even told me he was thinking about going back to junior college because she was going to enroll there for a year before going on to a state school. He even said they might get married. But then she started breaking up with him all the time. I couldn't figure out why. Then one day I ran into her at a restaurant in a mall and she told me everything. She was only nineteen and she just wasn't ready for the kind of commitment my brother wanted. She said they'd agree not to talk about marriage but then the subject always came up and he'd get angry and she'd get scared."

"Was he ever violent with her?"

"No. She said that wasn't what scared her. She had the same fear I did, that he'd take his own life. She was afraid to break it off completely because of that but she couldn't deal with Neil anymore, either. Then she said something that I've never forgotten. Neil told her that the only time he didn't have nightmares was when things were going well with them. Then I realized how dependent he was on her. She made him feel good again—much better than the army counselor in Nam he saw who just kind of ran him through his office once a month. I sympathized with her. And Jenny was a sweet girl. She told me that she'd decided that the easiest way out was to go to the University of Illinois for freshman year and leave in a week.

"She went and that's when the trouble really started. He lost his job, he gave his best friend a black eye, and he swung on a cop who was trying to arrest him for drunk and disorderly. He managed to escape, and that's when he disappeared for a while. I was the only one he contacted. He knew if he came back he'd have to go to county jail or maybe even prison and he said he couldn't do it. But I convinced him he couldn't keep running like that. I got him a good lawyer. He served six months in county in Illinois. After he got out he drifted to Iowa City and that's where he met Richard. Richard invited him to live at the commune. Neil got a job in town working at a discount store. I'd just graduated college and had free time so I came here to live in the commune and try to straighten him out. He'd already been seeing Vanessa Mainwaring. I met her a few times and liked her. I think Neil had learned about not pushing too hard. They seemed very happy together. Then they had this argument. I never knew what it was about. I guess they started shouting at each other on Mainwaring's front lawn and he came out and told Neil to go home. Apparently he'd liked Neil up to that point, but you see somebody shouting at your daughter, you're going to defend her."

"How long after that was she murdered?"

"Two nights."

I asked the question she didn't want to hear. "Do you know where he is right now?"

"No."

"If you knew, would you tell me?"

"No. And please don't give me any speeches. I don't want to be the one responsible for the police finding him. I know he didn't kill her."

"Does that mean that you have proof?"

"It means I know my brother."

I said it again. "If he's on the run and they catch him and he won't give up, he might get himself killed."

"You think I haven't thought of that?"

Harry Renwick knocked softly twice, then opened the door. "Time's up, Sam." He walked over to where Sarah sat. "We'll get you out of those cuffs."

The smile was unexpected. "He means once he gets me back to my cell."

"Best I can do, Miss."

"Tell Sykes that I'm officially her lawyer, will you, Harry?"

"Sure. He figured you would be. Oh—he's pretty mad about you saying John Wayne was a draft dodger."

"It's true."

"Yeah, I read that in the newspaper a long time ago. I decided I'd better not bring that up to the chief. You know how he feels about John Wayne."

Sarah Powers seemed lost. She glanced around the room. A man told me once that the only time he'd been in jail the whole experience was like a nightmare. This was county, not even hard time, and he only did thirty days for a drunk driving charge. He said all those prison movies were fake. They never dealt with how oppressive it was to be forced to live with men who had spent their lives cheating, stealing, beating people. And enjoying it. That was what scared him the most. The way they bragged about it. Then, he said, there were the smells. He said there were even men who laughed about the smells. I wondered if Sarah was having a similar experience here. Yes, the jail was new, and yes, she obviously considered herself worldly and tough. But she was really just a middle-class woman terrified for her brother. And now, I suspected, terrified for herself.

Sarah Powers said, "I'm sorry about knocking you out."

I just nodded.

Harry Renwick had good radar. "I'll keep an eye on her for you, Sam."

I think she would have hugged him if she hadn't had the cuffs on. Now she had at least one friend here. My first cigarette was long gone. I lighted a second and let her take a deep drag. Then I handed Harry my nearly new pack. "These are hers."

"They sure are," he said, taking the Luckies from me.

6

Sunlight blasted me into temporary blindness as I walked from the station to my car. Only when I was halfway there did I see the three people standing two cars from mine: Paul Mainwaring, his daughter Nicole, and Tommy Delaney. Delaney was a local high school football hero and former boyfriend of Vanessa.

He had a little kid's face—all red hair and freckles and pug nose—set atop an NFL body. In his black Hawkeye T-shirt you could see why he was so feared on the field. He started toward me, but Paul Mainwaring himself put a halting hand on his shoulder.

The car I referred to happened to be a new white four-door Jaguar.

I usually found myself defending Paul Mainwaring. For all his work with the military and inventing things vital to war—he was a prominent military engineer—he had a true interest in helping the poor and had given thousands of dollars to the local soup kitchen and church relief funds. The irony wasn't lost on me; I'd always wondered if it was lost on him.

The face he showed now, as he broke from the group and walked toward me, stunned me. The white button-down shirt, the chinos, and the white tennis shoes spoke of the preppy he would always be. The silver hair was disheveled for once. The sunken, bruised eye sockets and the unshaven cheeks and jaws revealed a man lost in not only despair but confusion. Even his walk was uncertain.

Tommy Delaney broke in front of him, aiming himself directly at me.

"Tommy, get back there where you belong."

Tommy gave me the practiced look that probably made even the toughest kids in high school run when he turned it on them. I just watched him as he fell into sulking. Behind him, Mainwaring's daughter Nicole started sobbing and put her hands to her face. I was embarrassed to be in Mainwaring's presence. I'd had the young man thought to be the killer of his daughter and I'd lost him because I wasn't clever enough to outthink a twenty-two-year-old girl. I wanted to say something but I wasn't sure what that would be.

"Paul, I owe you an apology."

He brushed it away. "It wasn't your fault, Sam. Don't listen to all this. I was in the army for four years. Things just go wrong sometimes. The girl admitted that she struck you on the back of the head with a steel rod and knocked you out. I don't know anybody who could stand up to that."

I wanted him to repeat what he'd just said. I couldn't quite believe it after just one hearing. I was already known as the man who'd been outsmarted by a young girl. It was absurd—as Paul said, anybody can be felled by a steel rod smashing into your skull—but when you have enemies they work with what they're given. And yet the one who should despise me the most for my stupidity was telling me that getting smacked in the head was the reason I wasn't able to arrest Neil Cameron. Not because I was incompetent.

"I let myself down, Paul."

He extended his hand and we shook. I wasn't sure why we shook.

Then he offered his second surprise. "I want to hire you, Sam."

I allowed myself the luxury of a smile. "Right. I can see that. I come highly recommended."

"As I said, things happen. You've done some good work as a private investigator. And you know all the kids out at that commune. If anybody knows where Cameron might have gone, they do."

"I'm not sure they trust me."

"They trust you more than they do Cliffie. I've asked him a number of times to stop harassing them but all I get are those speeches Reverend Cartwright gives. All the marijuana and sex. By now Cliffie must've run every one of them in at least once. They certainly won't cooperate with him."

"I'm representing Sarah Powers, Paul. You should know that up front."

He blinked only once. "I didn't know that."

"That's why I think you should look for somebody else."

"She of course says Neil didn't kill Van."

"That's what she says."

"And you believe her?"

"In a case like this I only represent people I think are innocent. I want to find Neil and have him turn himself in."

"What if he's guilty?"

"Then he's guilty. If he's not, then I want to find the person who really killed Van."

"Then there's no conflict. I still want to hire you."

"I wish you'd think it over. I can recommend a few people in Cedar Rapids or even Des Moines. It might be better to let them handle it instead of me."

For the first time I saw resentment—anger—in the long, angular face. "You have a stake in this now, too, Sam. You need to prove to people you're not the fool they say you are."

He'd meant for his words to hurt. He'd succeeded. "I'll send a check to your office. I appreciate this, Sam." He spoke through a kind of pain I'd never had to deal with. "Maybe I'll call you tomorrow."

He turned and walked back to his people and his Jag. His daughter came to him and slid her arm around his waist. She tilted her head against his chest as he guided her to their car.

Tommy walked a few feet toward me and said, "Hope no girls beat you up on the way home, McCain."

"Get back here," Mainwaring shouted without turning around.

Of course Tommy gave me the famous soul-freezing evil eye before he did what Mainwaring said. I wondered what he'd look like if I was fortunate enough to back over him six or seven times.

A few years ago, before Jamie married her wastrel boyfriend Turk and bore him a baby girl as sweet as Jamie herself, I always checked out the clothes she wore. She had one of those stunning bodies you see on the covers of paperbacks, usually under the title *Teenage Tease* or some such thing. The wholesome pretty face only made her more appealing. These days I checked her for signs of bruises and cuts. In the first year of their marriage Turk had given her a black eye. I returned the favor by giving Turk a black eye. I'm not tough, but I'm tougher than Turk. I also drew up divorce papers that Jamie refused to sign. She loved him and he would change, she said.

These days I had her solemn word that if he ever got physically violent with her again she was to tell me immediately. I made her promise on her mother's life. A good Catholic girl, she took such oaths seriously.

Turk still had his surfing band, probably the only one in landlocked Iowa—despite the fact that surfing bands were now seen as wimpy and irrelevant. And he was still going to be on *American Bandstand*, though *American Bandstand* was fading fast. And he was still going to have several gold records. And he was still, when the time was right, planning to become a movie star. And he still didn't want to get a job because working conflicted with his songwriting and practicing. He couldn't even babysit his little daughter. That was left to Jamie's mother. These artistes, they need their time to create.

Today Jamie wore a sleeveless yellow blouse and a richer yellow miniskirt. She was easy to scan for bruises. I didn't see any. She also wore a pair of brown-rimmed eyeglasses. She'd started having headaches so I'd paid for her visit to an optometrist and then for the glasses. I still wondered about the headaches. I didn't trust Turk. Somehow in the course of our years together she'd become my little sister and I'd be goddamned if anybody was going to hurt her or baby Laurie.

Jamie's typing skills had improved marginally and she'd learned how to answer the phone professionally and take down information without mistakes. She gave me my messages and a cup of coffee. That was another thing she handled capably. Our new automatic coffee brewer. Me being me, I still couldn't make a decent cup of coffee, even with that new machine I'd bought on sale at Sears. But Jamie had triumphed.

As I went through my phone messages, I glanced up once and saw the way Jamie straightened all four of the framed photographs of one-year-old Laurie she had on her desk. Not that they needed straightening. But touching them brought her peace you could see in her face. At these times I always wanted to kill Turk. He should honor her for her sweetness and loyalty. Maybe I could get him convicted as a Russki spy and get him deported. After I beat the shit out of him.

7

In grade school we always swapped comic books. Kenny Thibodeau tended to like Superman and The Flash. I went more for Batman and Captain Marvel. In junior high we swapped paperbacks. Mickey Spillane and Richard S. Prather were early favorites though soon enough I discovered Peter Rabe and F. Scott Fitzgerald, among others. Kenny discovered John Steinbeck and Henry Miller. In high school I'd picked up on all the Gold Medal crime writers such as Charles Williams, while Kenny had discovered Jack Kerouac and the Beats. At none of these junctures was it possible to predict what Kenny would bring to the table—literally the table in the booth at Andy's Donuts where I'd gone straight from jail—on this already hot and humid morning.

Baby pictures.

His daughter Melissa was two and a half years old. She wasn't just the center of Kenny's life, she was *all* of Kenny's life. Yes, he still wrote his soft-core sex novels and he still wrote his men's magazine "Die

52

Nazi Die!" articles, but those he did almost unconsciously these days. Automatic pilot. His conscious attention was devoted to Melissa. All this was reflected in his attire. Not a vestige of the former Beat. Short, thinning brown hair. Pressed yellow short-sleeved cotton shirt and pressed brown trousers. I mention pressed by way of introducing his wife, Sue. As Kenny always joked, by marrying him Sue had inherited both a husband and a son. Kenny needed help and Sue, loving and amused, was there to provide it.

"This one's of Melissa and the cocker spaniel we got her last week."

Even though we had gone past picture number twenty I had to admit this one of Melissa in her frilly sundress leaning down to kiss the puppy on the head was pretty damned cute.

"And here's one—"

I held up my hand. "I don't mean to be rude, Kenny, but I've got a lot to do today."

For only a moment he looked hurt, then he grinned. "Yeah, Sue says I drive people nuts with my pictures. Just be glad I haven't invited you out to see the slide show I made of all the pictures we have of her."

"You have a slide show? Seriously?"

"With music." He sipped his coffee. "Don't worry, you'll get to see it one of these days."

"That sounds like a threat."

The timbre of his laugh hadn't changed since we were in fourth grade. "It is. But I'm sure you want to talk about the girl who got killed last night."

Kenny was the unofficial historian of Black River Falls for our generation. Every once in a while he'd talk about this huge novel he was going to write someday, a kind of *Peyton Place* about our own small city. Despite his reputation for writing smutty books, people liked Kenny and confided in him. He knew secrets nobody else did. He'd been helping me with cases since the day I'd hung out my shingle.

"Do you know anything about her?"

"I know one thing."

"What's that?"

"She's been seen with Bobby Randall on occasion."

"You're kidding."

"Wild child. Lot of trouble for her old man."

"Bobby Randall deals drugs."

"That's my point. A lot of trouble for her old man."

"I'm representing Sarah Powers. She's the sister of Neil Cameron, the guy everybody's looking for. They're both part of the commune. You ever hear of Bobby Randall hanging out at the commune?"

"Oh, sure. They had some real head-trippers out there for a while. Right after Donovan and the rest of them came here. Randall was the only source they had so they dealt with him. But finally the head-trippers moved on. Randall still goes out there. I think he had something going with one of the girls at the commune for a while, but she broke it off with him for some reason. He's a heartbreaker."

I took a moment to finish my glazed donut. This coffee shop was one of the few small businesses that hadn't shriveled up since the new mall opened. The larger downtown stores had all moved to the mall, taking with them a good deal of traffic and thus business. The mayor had been frothy with reassurances that the mall would increase business for everybody because shoppers who'd trekked to Iowa City or Cedar Rapids would now be happy to shop here again. The younger people thought it was pretty cool of course. But the older ones—and the ones like Wendy and me, touched by a spiritual old age on occasion—saw it as one of those generational betrayals that are a part of growing up. The young betray the old until they are old enough to be betrayed by the next generation. I'm sure the good Reverend Cartwright has an explanation for such things.

"You hear much about the Mainwaring family?"

"Just that it's sort of gone to hell since Mrs. Mainwaring died and Mainwaring married again. I know the Mainwaring kids really don't like her."

"She's pretty exotic."

"Yeah, and from what I hear not a real warm person. But she went to Smith and worked on the Bobby Kennedy campaign and drives a Jag. I know you like Mainwaring but he's really a snob. And I still don't understand how a guy who makes stuff for war can pretend to be such a liberal."

"You think he's pretending?"

"Don't you?"

"I'm not sure. Maybe he's just sort of blind to himself."

"I don't trust him. I was in a peace march in Iowa City last month and I saw him on the sidewalk talking to a guy I was pretty sure was a fed."

"How can you tell?"

"Didn't you read that article in *Esquire* about how the feds who check out peace marches dress? Short hair, T-shirts, and jeans. Hoover likes his boys to wear uniforms. And they all drive black Fords with blackwalls because Hoover gets a deal on them."

One thing about Kenny—he'd never met a conspiracy theory he didn't like. "Maybe he's changed things because of that article."

"I doubt it. I admit I'm being paranoid but I still don't trust Mainwaring. I mean his *business* is with the federal government." He checked his wristwatch. "Melissa's at her grandmother's right now. I had to leave her there while I went to have Alan check my blood pressure. He sure is a smart-ass."

"You should've heard him last night when he was sewing me up."

"He was always like that." He slid out of the booth. "We were too mature to act like that, as I remember."

"Right. All the times we both called his glasses Mount Palomars. Real mature."

As if I hadn't spoken, he said: "I'll have some new pictures of Melissa next time I see you."

I wanted to ask if that was a threat or a promise but I was too mature to do it.

My early boyhood was spent in the section just past the city limits called the Hills. This was where the poor white people lived. Even sociologists would have had a hard time defining the Hills because there were degrees of poverty even here. Depending on where you lived in the Hills, your home was either lower-class livable or little more than a shack. If you lived in one of the shacks, which far out-numbered the tiny one- and two-bedroom homes, you saw a lot of the local gendarmes. A fair number of men dealt in stolen property; a fair number of men couldn't seem to stay out of bloody fights; and a fair number of men let the bottle keep them from steady jobs. In the midst of all this the more reliable people like my parents and many others tried to carry on respectable lives. Kenny lived in one of the shacks but was saved and redeemed by his early interest in books. My mother and father were both readers, Dad with his pulps and paper-backs and Mom with her magazines (one of them, *The American*, car-ried Nero Wolfe stories frequently, introducing me to mystery fiction around age eight or so), and encouraged my brother and sister to be readers as well.

The worst part of my early life was when my older brother Robert died of polio. He had been, no other word, my idol, all the things I could only hope to be. When I got old enough I drove his 1936 Plymouth. My sister Ruth was sure that Robert visited her at night in ghost form. And I remember hearing my father half whispering to my uncle Al that he was worried about my mother, that maybe she would never get over it and be herself again. We still went back to the Hills to lay fresh flowers on my brother's grave in the cemetery where Hills people buried their dead. In the worst of my depression after losing the woman I was sure would be my wife, I found myself waking one birdsong morning next to his gravestone. I had drunkenly confided in my brother—for that matter I'm not quite sure I ever really got over his death either—hoping he'd bring me solace.

Tommy Delaney lived in one of the small houses, this one iso-lated by the fact that it sat on a corner. Where there should have been neighbors on the west side of his place there were only three empty tracts. The city had made an effort to destroy the worst of the houses and shacks.

I heard the voices before I'd quite closed my car door. Man and woman; husband and wife. The ugly noise of marriage gone bad. There had been a time after Robert's death when my parents had gone at each other. As I later learned in my psych classes at the U of Iowa, this was not an uncommon reaction to the loss of a child. But their rages terrified my little sister and me. I'd take her to her tiny room and give her her doll and cover her with a blanket, anything to stop her sobbing. I'd sit on the bed till she went to sleep. They always promised, in whispers, that they'd never do it again. But they did of course. They were too aggrieved over the loss of their son not to.

The Delaney home was the size of a large garage but not as tall. The once-white clapboard was stained so badly it resembled wounds. The eaves on one side dangled almost to the ground. The two cement steps had pulled a few inches away from the front door. In addition to the screaming, a dog inside started barking, explaining the dog shit on the sunburnt grass. But not even a dog could compete with the cutting words of the argument.

There was a rusted doorbell. I tried it. Somewhere, faintly, it chimed. Not that this deterred the screamers. Either they hadn't heard it or they didn't care that they had company.

The door opened and there Tommy Delaney stood, massive in his Black River Warriors black T-shirt with the familiar yellow logo. He wiped the back of his hand across his eyes but he was too late. I could see he'd been crying, the same way my sister had always cried when our parents had played gladiators over the body of their oldest son.

Then he suddenly stepped on the concrete stairs. His weight was enough to make them wobble. I backed down to the ground. He reached back and jerked the door shut. That was when I noticed the tic in his left eye. Kids respond differently to parental warfare. The big tough football player had developed a tic. He'd probably developed other problems, too, ones less obvious.

He blushed. Blood went up his cheeks like a rising elevator. "They're just havin' a little disagreement." The tic got worse. Heavy fingers pawed at it as if they could destroy it.

"How about walking over to my car? Maybe it'll be easier to talk there." It wouldn't be—not with this battle going on—but at least we wouldn't be right next to it.

"I don't know what you're doing here."

"I'm trying to find out who murdered your friend Vanessa."

"You *know* who murdered her."

"I know who people *think* murdered her. That doesn't mean they're right."

The baby face sagged in the brutal light of a ninety-two-degree day. For all his power, he looked drained. I doubted he'd slept much. "You stick up for the hippies. I always told her not to go out there. I told her there'd be trouble. Neil Cameron was crazy. You should read some of the letters he wrote her. He belonged in a bughouse."

"Tell me about the letters."

The tic had slowed some. I had to give his parents one thing— they had the strength of boxers who could go fifteen rounds easy. If anything, they were louder than ever.

"I only read a couple of them. But they were nuts."

"That doesn't tell me anything about the letters."

"Just the way he said stuff. That he'd kill himself if she didn't come back to him. And that they had this sacred bond that couldn't be broken. And that sometimes he stood on her street late at night staring up at her bedroom window and that he thought about just getting a ladder and kidnapping her."

His father shouted a particularly ugly word at his mother. Delaney glanced over his shoulder. When he turned back to me he resembled a little boy who had just heard something terrible but mystifying. Maybe his father had never used that particular word before. The tic got bad again.

"Sorry you have to listen to that."

"Yeah, why would you give a shit?"

"Maybe because I heard things like that for a while myself when I was young."

"Yeah, well—" He swiped his hand across the tic again. But for the first time agitation left his eyes.

"You know the Mainwaring family."

"Not for much longer. I think Mainwaring's going to tell me he doesn't want me there anymore. He liked the idea of a football hero hanging around his place but I think the novelty's worn off."

He was smarter and shrewder than I'd given him credit for. "Were you in love with Vanessa?"

"What the hell kind of question is that? It's none of your damned business." Then: "For your information, I thought I was but when I saw how she treated me and every other guy around her, I just enjoyed the free ride and let her go her own way."

"What free ride?"

A smile loaded with malice. He angled himself toward the house where the spiritual murder was taking place. "The free ride of staying in a mansion where there was peace and quiet and eating better than I ever had. They even have a maid. All you have to do is say you want a Pepsi or a piece of pie and she goes and gets it for you. They even have guest rooms. It's like staying in a nice hotel. Mainwaring let me stay overnight any time I wanted to, and I wanted to a lot."

I waited a moment before asking my next question. We just stared at each other. Then I said: "All I'm asking is one favor. I want you to think about who might have wanted Vanessa dead besides Neil Cameron."

"He killed her. You know it and I know it."

"I don't know it, Delaney. But I'd appreciate it if you'd think about it and give me a call." I handed him a card.

As he studied the card, the shrill got shriller in the house behind us. He shuddered. His entire upper body just shook for ten seconds or so. Then he sighed: "Maybe I'll think about it. Maybe not. Right now I've gotta get back in there before it gets any worse." He made a face. "I have nightmares he's gonna kill her sometime."

Then he was gone, trotting across the dead brown grass to the hell house.

8

"Was Jesus a hippie? I think not. Did Jesus smoke pot? Did Jesus listen to the Rolling Stones? Did Jesus burn the American flag? No, he didn't. And Jesus never said vile things about the Vietnam War, either."

Reverend Cartwright's midday radio show.

It wasn't really a manor house but it tried to be, a three-story native stone building of twenty-five rooms, nine baths, and two dining rooms, not to mention a fireplace that you could walk into. Not while logs were burning, of course. The home lay on fifteen acres of green trimmed lawn with gasp-inducing hedges and stone-edged ponds on which swans swam, and pines of such sweet perfume you got dizzy. Behind the house was the bright red barn where Eve Mainwaring had the six horses she ran in her white-fenced three-acre domain. All four doors of the garage were open, revealing the fact that Mainwaring didn't think much of American car making. There was a Porsche, two Mercedes sedans, and a Jaguar. All of recent vintage.

I'd called ahead. Mainwaring had told me to come around to the back veranda where he was having lunch. The day was well on its way to reaching the predicted ninety. From an open upstairs window I heard The Byrds' version of Bob Dylan's "Tambourine Man." As I looked up I saw a young female face, framed by long dark hair, watching me. The youngest of the Mainwarings, Nicole. She leaned back, out of sight.

Mainwaring sat beneath a large blue umbrella at a table of glass and chrome. He appeared to be staring out at the swimming pool. The water was blue and chemically fresh, no doubt. It was also empty.

I was still behind him when he said, "She always swam in the mornings. When it got cold she swam indoors. She rarely missed a morning."

I didn't have to ask who he was talking about. I walked across the fieldstone veranda and seated myself at his table. It was cooler under the umbrella. He wore a starched white short-sleeved button-down shirt, tan military-style walking shorts, white socks, and white tennis shoes. Before him was a plate that held two halves of an English muffin and two poached eggs. One half of the muffin, covered with strawberry jam, had been nibbled on. The eggs hadn't been touched. They looked like the eyes of a comic monster. Next to his coffee cup lay his package of Chesterfields. "I don't eat breakfast. I run three miles and then have breakfast for lunch."

I wasn't sure what to say. Good for you or tell him how my day starts. You know, peeing and having a cigarette as soon as possible. But that doesn't sound quite as impressive as a three-mile run, I guess.

There were no amenities.

"I wanted you to talk to Nicole, Sam. But she and I had a disagreement this morning so she's up in her room sulking." He took a long drag on his cigarette. In the shade of the umbrella his silver hair didn't glow quite as much. "Eve will be joining us in a few minutes."

He paused. His harsh blue eyes showed pain. "She was what we were arguing about, of course. Neither of the girls accepted her. They never gave her a chance."

"That's a tough transition sometimes. A stepmother."

"They never gave her a chance."

I was expected to agree with him.

"I see."

Then, appearing in the French doors behind us, was a sight rare even in the upper-class homes of our town. A maid, a real one, in a gray uniform and everything. White and fiftyish and from the looks of her, Irish. If she spoke with a brogue I'd suspect that we'd been transported into a sitcom.

"Will there be anything else, Mr. Mainwaring? I need to get going on the laundry."

"Marsha, this is Sam McCain. He'll be working with me for a while. Have you had lunch, Sam?"

I lied. "I have, yes. But I'd appreciate some coffee."

"Why don't you bring us a fresh pot, Marsha?"

"Sure. Anything else, Mr. McCain?"

"No. But thanks for asking."

After Marsha had left, Mainwaring said, "You're like I was at first. Nervous about having somebody wait on me all the time. Marsha was Eve's idea. Ironically, the girls like Marsha much more than they do Eve."

I didn't correct the tense he was using. It was difficult to get it right when one daughter was alive and the other one was dead.

"Have you started work yet, Sam?"

A breeze carried the scent of the water in the pool. I was trying to say the unsayable. "I've been trying to get some background on Vanessa."

Paul Mainwaring's eyes narrowed and a bitter smile crossed his face. "Then you know she was something of a tease. Maybe even something of a whore."

Fathers aren't supposed to say that about their daughters. Other people say it and fathers say you're a g.d. liar.

"That's a little harsh."

"No, it's not, unfortunately. She was a very nice young girl even after her mother died. She was an A student, helped around the house and spent a lot of time making sure that Nicole and I were all right. I sent her to a counselor just to make sure that she wasn't hiding any deep problems. I was afraid that maybe she was really depressed but covering it up. The counselor said she was a remarkably mature fifteen-year-old and that she was dealing with Donna's death very well. All that changed when I brought Eve here and told the girls that I was getting married to her. They didn't even pretend to like her. We had the wedding here. The girls went somewhere else. Wouldn't come under any circumstances. In fact they stayed at their aunt's in Cedar Rapids for two weeks before they came back. And it was right after that that Vanessa started changing. It was very conscious on her part. She got into the whole hippie thing. Didn't wear a bra. I could smell the pot in her room. She also started bringing boys up to her room, something I'd never allowed before. I found some unused Trojans on her desk one day. She'd left them there on purpose so I'd be sure to see them. She wanted me to see them. She wanted to hurt me."

"What was Nicole doing all this time?"

This time the smile was fond. "Little Nicole? She did what she always did, followed her sister. She got the same clothes and listened to the same music and started spouting the same rhetoric. It was sort of sweet in an odd way. Vanessa would be going on about capitalism and how the pigs had taken over—I was of course one of the pigs. They used to be proud that I'd made my own way in the world and had become wealthy doing it. But now I was a pig. A liberal pig. But I was saying it was sweet—and it was. Vanessa had some idea of what she was talking about when she argued about the capitalist system. But Nicole—she was this innocent little girl with all these big words and big concepts and she had no idea what she was talking about."

"And where did Eve fit into all this?"

"Eve did the best she could under the circumstances, but obviously it wasn't enough."

63

The words had come from behind the sheer white curtains covering the French doors. Eve appeared in her jodhpurs and white silk blouse. Her brown leather riding boots gleamed. "I only listened for the last few minutes. I thought that since I heard my name mentioned I might as well join you."

She was the sort of woman you saw in *The New Yorker* or *Town & Country*, ruthlessly fashionable and relentlessly beautiful in a cold, poised fashion. The one thing she couldn't control were the age lines that had begun to mar her elegant features. The closer she came, the less intimidating she was. Her weapon's edge was being dulled by time. She understood this. She took the chair furthest from me to sit in, blond hair gleaming in its chignon, a bit oversprayed so that you'd be forgiven for mistaking it for a wig.

She reached over and took her husband's hand. "Thank you for sticking up for me, darling." To me she said: "This is why I married him. This is the worst moment of his life—even worse than losing Donna, I think—and he's still generous enough to defend me."

She talked in sudsy prose, like soap opera talk, and I didn't like her at all. When Marsha appeared with our pot of coffee and two cups, Eve snapped, "Don't I usually have coffee with my husband, Marsha? You only brought two cups."

Marsha was wise. She wanted to keep her job. "I'll bring you a cup right away."

"And food. I assume you made lunch for me. I do need food, you know."

Marsha looked at me. She had no trouble reading the distaste in my eyes. It matched the distaste in hers. "I made roast beef sandwiches, a fruit salad, and a lettuce salad. I'll bring them out."

When she was gone, Mainwaring said, "She does her best, Eve."

"She's local. That's the problem. I wish you'd let me bring in somebody from Chicago."

"I know her husband. He works in my plant here. I couldn't face him every day if I fired her. Besides, I like her."

How strange it was, I thought, that Eve had managed to shift the conversation from the heartbreak of a young girl's murder to some goddamn maid problem—which wasn't a problem after all, Marsha being somebody I'd taken to right away. Apparently, on an astronomical chart, in the center of the universe you would find a planet named Eve.

"I'd like to get back to Vanessa."

"Of course, Sam. I'm sorry."

"So the girls and Eve didn't get along."

"Eve did everything she could."

"All right. But because of her—blameless as she was—" Her eyes pinched as I said this. Had she heard the slight irony in my voice? "Blameless as she was, Vanessa rebelled and started going around with too many guys."

"Sleeping with too many guys. You may as well say it, Sam."

"And taking drugs."

That froze both of them in their chairs.

"Where did you hear that?"

"I'm investigating, Paul. I see people. I ask questions."

"You may as well tell him, Paul. Vanessa was a dope addict."

She was a few decades behind in her drug slang but that didn't diminish the pleasure she took—and tried unsuccessfully to hide—in confirming what I'd said.

Paul's face grayed with her remark. I wondered if he was going to be sick. "If that's the way you want to put it, Eve."

But she was the dutiful and cunning wife. She took his hand in both of hers and said—her first show of warmth—"Oh God, honey, that came out much harsher than I meant it. I'm sorry."

He was all forgiveness; color returned to his cheeks. "Oh, don't mind me. It's just a hard thing to face. You didn't mean anything by it." He eased his hand from between hers. His gaze was that of a teenager wistfully tending to his first love. "I don't know what I'd do without you, honey."

I remembered Donna, the mother of his two children. She'd been small, tending to plumpishness, and very much a housewife and a member of such organizations as the PTA and the League of Women Voters. If Eve had a polar opposite, Donna had been it. Had Mainwaring spent his married life pining for the bed of a beauty? Or had he, with his money and his importance, decided that it was time he got a show woman for a wife?

"What did you and Vanessa argue about, Mrs. Mainwaring?"

"I wasn't aware that we *did* argue."

"That's being a little harsh, Sam. They didn't have arguments most of the time—they just sort of froze her out."

"I see."

"Is this how you conduct most of your investigations?"

"Now don't get your back up, Eve. He's just doing his job."

"Well," Eve said, "then he can do his job without me."

She was on her feet, all jodhpur'd and indignant. "I'm sorry, Paul, but I'm not in the mood for this. Vanessa and I had our differences but that doesn't mean I didn't love her and consider her my own flesh and blood."

She had a line of shit that stretched from Iowa to Montana. But she was polished and just good enough at the acting to pass muster if you had the misfortune to be in love with her. Obviously the kids had identified her species as soon as they met her.

Katharine Hepburn had never walked out of a scene with more mannered disdain.

"I don't know why you had to make her mad, Sam. Maybe this isn't a good fit. I still can't believe my daughter's dead and now I've got my wife mad at me."

"I can quit or you can fire me. But the question I asked her was legitimate. You said yourself that she and your kids didn't get along. I wanted to get her take on things."

He leaned back in his chair and closed his eyes. "All the arguments I had with Vanessa in the last couple of years—I wish I could take every one of them back." The purity of sorrow was now being tainted with remorse, making it all the worse for him. I said nothing. There was nothing to say.

Marsha appeared bearing a large glass tray. "Where's the missus?"

I wondered how Eve would like being known as "the missus." It didn't go with anyone who wore jodhpurs.

Mainwaring opened his eyes and sat up straight. "Eve had some business she had to take care of right away." The smile was strained. "This looks delicious, as usual. Thank you very much."

Marsha glanced at me for some explanation about why Eve had left so suddenly and why he'd been sitting with his eyes closed. I shook my head. She shrugged and said, "If you need anything more, just let me know."

"Thanks, Marsha."

After she was gone, Mainwaring said, "I'll handle Eve. She'll give me a raft of shit about you but she'll get over it. She's a very private person."

"I can always apologize to her if you'd like."

"No, no, I'd better handle it myself. She's very sensitive. Her parents were wealthy people who died in a plane crash when she was seven. She went to a convent school in Paris until she was nineteen and then she came over here and went to Smith. She eventually taught English literature at Dartmouth. So she's very worldly. But she still gets defensive whenever the subject of the girls comes up. They made things very tough for her. And now you'll be investigating and bringing back a lot of bad memories for her."

I poured myself some coffee. "There's no other way to do it. Those memories will be important." I sipped the coffee. Marsha might be local but she sure knew how to make good coffee. "I have another question for you right now."

"You don't quit, do you?"

"I'd be wasting your money if I did."

"Fair enough."

"Do you know a young man named Bobby Randall?"

"That bastard. I threatened to kill him one night. I had half a mind to do it, too. Right out on our drive he sold Vanessa some drugs. A small envelope. When I saw what was happening I ran out there. Vanessa stopped me from hitting him, otherwise I would've pounded him into the ground. All he did was smirk at me. That was when I lost control. I almost knocked Vanessa down getting to him but then she started screaming at me so I finally calmed down. That punk was still smirking."

"You didn't call Cliffie?"

"How could I? If I had, he'd have arrested Vanessa, too. She'd never have forgiven me if I'd done anything like that."

He was a compromised man, beholden to both his children and the wife his children despised. Either way he moved, he was going to make somebody unhappy. There was a plea in his voice when he said, "And now I'm worried about Nicole. I don't want her to turn out the way Van did."

As Marsha led me through the house and to the front door, she spoke softly. "I sure hope you can help him." She looked around. I knew what she was going to say. "His new wife won't, that's for sure." Now she put her mouth close to my ear. "I'm pretty sure she's happy that Vanessa's dead. Now all she'll have to worry about is Nicole."

I wasn't paying attention when I made my way to my car. I was sorting through some of the things I'd heard inside. When I focused on where I was going, I was surprised to see Nicole sitting in my front seat on the passenger side.

I got in and closed the door.

It was always said that Vanessa was the beauty and Nicole the brain. Nice and tidy, but not true. Nicole was a nice-looking seventeen-year-old whose problem was acne. I went through a year of bad acne myself so I still had nightmares occasionally of waking up and feeling my face only to find that it was once again corrugated. She was kin to Sarah Powers, Neil Cameron's sister. Their high school years had to have been hell.

Today she wore a white blouse and blue walking shorts. She held a can of Coke in one hand and a burning Winston in the other. "She's watching us."

"Who?"

"The bitch. Eve."

"How do you know?"

"See that window to the right of the east dormer?"

"Yeah."

"Watch the curtain. It'll move."

I watched. She was right.

"Why would she watch?"

"She always watches. Van and I always joked she was a spy." She made a face suddenly, leaned forward in the seat.

"Are you all right, Nicole?"

Her fingers touched her sweaty forehead. "It's just everything that's happening, I guess." She took a deep breath. "What were we talking about?"

"You don't get along with Eve?"

"You met my real mother."

"Yes, many times. She was a very good woman."

"Well, compare her to Eve and see why we hated her so much."

I didn't say anything.

A cruel smile. "I was listening to you on the veranda. The bitch even cut into you, too. She should've died instead of Van."

"Your father's in love with her."

"I know. That's what's so sickening. We met two or three of his lady friends, you know, after Mom died. They were all nice women. We would have been happy if he'd married one of them, but then Eve came along."

"How did they meet?"

"Some party in Iowa City. She was going out with this art teacher there. She dumped him right away, of course. Dad has a lot more money."

The way her fingers touched her ravaged face I could tell she'd become aware of me watching her carefully. But she'd misinterpreted why I was watching her. Beneath the scarring was an innocent, appealing face that made it seem impossible that she could be capable of so much anger.

"We used to plot how to get rid of her."

"Anything ever come of it?"

She smiled for the first time. "We were chicken." Then: "God, poor Van. I try not to think about it but it doesn't work. I barely slept last night." She picked up the cigarette she'd put in the ashtray. "I'd never say this to my father but I even feel sorry for Neil."

"You got to know him?"

"Sure. Dad liked him and Marsha liked him and I liked him. Eve didn't. She's such a snotty bitch. She always told Van she shouldn't go out with 'lower-class boys.' Van used to laugh about that. It's not like we're living in New York or anything. There are rich people here but it's not like there's this big deal when it comes to dating. Everybody goes to public school and goes out with everybody else." She put her knees up against the dashboard and slumped in the seat and tapped out another cigarette for herself.

I disagreed with her about the town not having a class system but I doubted that people talked about it as crudely as Eve had put it.

"And Van thought she was seeing somebody on the side." She lit her cigarette, inhaled, exhaled.

"That's a pretty heavy accusation. What made Van think so?"

"She said one time when Dad was out of town she caught Eve and the handyman looking guilty when they were coming out of that cabana by the pool. She said Eve hurried over to her and was real friendly. Eve's never real friendly."

"Who's the handyman?"

"You know a guy named Bobby Randall?"

Bobby Randall—handyman. I'd forgotten that. He was an excellent carpenter as well. "Yeah, I do."

"Well, he's real good-looking and he knows it. Van—" She glanced out the window before speaking. "Van was into drugs. Heavy stuff sometimes. I stick to pot. Anyway, Van got her drugs from Bobby. He was always trying to get her into bed. She led him on—she did that a lot. People said she slept around and I guess that was true. But a lot of it was just kind of leading them on. Playing with them. She did it to hurt our dad. You know, because of that bitch Eve. I would've done the same thing probably if I didn't have—" She flipped her cigarette out the window and brought her knees down from the dashboard. "You know, my problems." The fingers of her left hand went— unconsciously?—to her cheek.

She opened the door. "The curtains just moved again up in Eve's room."

I said, "You've done a good job of convincing me not to like her. I didn't take to her right off but you clinched the deal."

She offered a slender hand and a smile. "Good. Then we're friends."

As we shook, I said, "We sure are."

Then, softly, she said: "Why couldn't it have been Eve instead of Van?"

She pushed herself out of the car with her foot and jogged back to the mansion.

9

"Would you like half my sandwich, Mr. C? It's bigger than I thought it would be."

"I'm not really hungry, Jamie. Why don't you eat what you want and then stick the rest in the little refrigerator down the hall and take it home tonight."

"Turk doesn't like leftover stuff."

Well, since you're supporting the family while Turk is loafing, he should be grateful for any food he gets. If I didn't care for Jamie as much as I did, I would have erupted like that five times a day, every time she unwittingly revealed how Turk took advantage of her. They'd broken up a few years ago because he'd had another girlfriend on the side. The marriage had been called off. But gradually she'd weakened under all his promises to be the man—or punk, in my estimation—he knew he could be. Her parents couldn't pay for the small, informal wedding so I made a present of picking up the tab. I also got her on a decent low-cost insurance plan because I knew she'd be pregnant soon enough. She'd confided to me through tears—this when she'd discovered Turk's girlfriend—that Turk didn't care for rubbers. At that moment her period was late and she was terrified. The period came a few days later. I put Turk on the same insurance plan only because she pleaded with me. I had dreams of running him down with my car just to see how reliable the insurance coverage was.

"Aw, what the hey, Jamie, I'll take half your sandwich."

"I always like it when we eat together here. It's real homey."

Turk, you son of a bitch, if you ever hurt her again I'll tear your throat out.

The pastrami on rye she'd gotten from Goldblatt's deli down the street was excellent as always. We mostly talked about her baby. Jamie was starting a college fund that she was keeping secret from good old Turk because he "sometimes" tended to spend every cent in the house. She said that she wanted her baby to be a doctor or a lawyer—"just like you, Mr. C."

Then the two phone lines started buzzing and it was back to work.

Without quite knowing why, I called the Wilhoyt Investigative Agency in Chicago. This was a prominent firm that had recently helped bring down a powerful and corrupt politician who fought every civil rights bill that came up, despite the fact that he had a Negro mistress. He didn't seem to understand the incongruity. He must have thought he was back running the plantation.

My contact at Wilhoyt was an older man named Pete Federman. He'd hired me four times to work on cases he was overseeing in Iowa City and Cedar Rapids. The checks were about double what I charged here. Federman had a cigarette hack and a lot of jokes about what it was like living under the burden of being a Cubs fan.

"You see the game yesterday, McCain?"

"Couple innings on TV."

"I'm taking a cyanide capsule with me next time I go. They screw up like they did yesterday, I'll just slide it under my tongue and that'll be that. The way my oldest boy's been carryin' on, that doesn't sound all that bad anyway." Hack. "So what can I do for you?"

I told him about Eve. Gave him all the details about her background I'd managed to put together.

"If this isn't all bullshit she must be quite the doll."

I told him about Vanessa's death. "The girls couldn't stand her. After talking to her this morning it was easy to see why."

"Solid gold bitch, huh?"

"Yeah, and one who seems to enjoy the role."

"I'll probably need twenty-four hours on this. I take it you're on an expense account."

"Yeah."

"Then no discounts. For you personally I'd go twenty-five percent off."

"Hey, I appreciate that."

"You do good work, kid."

"Well, you do good work, too, Pete."

The big agencies had access to people and documentation all over the country. The starting point would probably be Dartmouth, where she'd been a professor. They'd likely work backward from there.

I'd been talking on line one. As soon as I began lowering the receiver, line two rang. Jamie answered, "Sam McCain's law office." She sounded official as hell. She listened and then said: "He's right here, Commander Potter." She nodded to me. I picked up; she hung up.

"Hi, Mike, what's going on?"

"You know that old Skelly station near the roundhouse? Been closed down for a couple years?"

"Sure. Why?"

"Well, somebody spotted Cameron there and I jumped in the car and found him."

"You bringing him in?"

"Yeah, Sam. But there isn't any hurry. He put a .45 to his head and killed himself."

74

PART TWO

10

The station had been abandoned in the late '40s, the reason being that the ones in town were new and bright and easy to get to. This was a holdover from the early '30s, a two-pump station that sold only gas and oil, no car repairs. Kids had smashed out the windows and animals had used the drive as a bathroom. The front door had been chained shut. If you looked through one of the dust-coated front windows you could see a large movie poster advertising a Betty Grable film circa 1945 when Betty was already slipping in popularity.

Three squad cars and an ambulance were parked on the east side of the station. I pulled up behind them and walked to the back of the place where a green wooden storage shed was tucked into a stand of hardwoods. Potter was explaining to two uniforms how he wanted them to gather evidence, who would start where, and so on. The ambulance boys leaned against the open rear doors of their big white box, looking slightly bored and taking it out on their cigarettes. As usual, the joyous birdsong reminded me that the so-called lower orders could give a shit about the travails of the plodding creatures that lumbered across their land. Nature presented them with their own travails.

Potter set his men to work and then walked over to me. "I'd let you have a look at him but we're still gathering evidence. I wanted you out here so I could tell you firsthand what I saw when *I* got out here. He's in the back of the shed. He had a blanket and some sandwiches in a brown paper bag. Obviously somebody helped him. From what I could see, he didn't have any marks on his arms or hands or face. No signs of a struggle, in other words, in case you're thinking somebody killed him and then planted the gun in his hand. He fired a .45 above his right ear. The exit wound is a big bastard, bigger than usual. The doc is on his way. He'll be able to guesstimate when Cameron did the deed. Now, I'm sure you have a lot of questions, so if you want to wait around for a couple of hours—there's a pretty good burger joint about a mile from here—we'll probably have a lot more information for you."

"I'm sure your boss will take this as an admission of guilt."

"Right now I do, Sam. And if you can step back and be a little objective, you should, too. You'll say everything's circumstantial and it probably is, but he was obsessed with the girl, she broke it off with him, and he killed her. That's not exactly a new story. He hides out, he's afraid and probably sorry for what he'd done, and he kills himself."

"Where did he get the gun?"

"Where did he get the sandwiches and the blanket? Probably the same place."

"I'll get to see the blanket and gun?"

"As long as the chief isn't here. He's still pissed off about your John Wayne crack. Being a draft dodger and all."

"Good thing I didn't tell him that Superman can't actually fly."

He shook his head and smiled. "You two really hate each other, don't you?"

"I don't hate him as much as he hates me."

"Yeah, I kind of figured that was the case." He waved to a squad car that had just pulled up. "Now I gotta get back to work."

I drove back to town. When I saw a phone booth outside a Howard Johnson's I pulled over. I had Paul Mainwaring's phone number scribbled in the small notepad I carry in my left back pocket. Marsha the maid answered.

"I'm afraid he's at the funeral home, Mr. McCain. The burial will be tomorrow. Mr. Mainwaring just wants to get it over with."

"Well, will you please give him this message, Marsha? The police have found Neil Cameron's body in a shed in back of that old Skelly station on the edge of town."

Her gasp—and it was indeed a gasp—surprised me. "Oh, my Lord."

"Are you all right, Marsha?"

"He was such a nice boy. I liked him so much."

She was reacting as if a close friend had died. "Did you know him pretty well, Marsha?"

"He was around here a lot. Sometimes Vanessa would invite him over, but by the time he'd get here some other boy would have picked her up and taken her off. I cared for Vanessa but she was very cruel to boys sometimes. He'd look so sad I'd talk to him. Every so often, if I wasn't busy and nobody else was around, I'd talk to him for quite a while. My own son is in his thirties and lives in Michigan with his family. I suppose I kind of adopted Neil a little bit. I know he was upset, but I don't for a minute believe he murdered poor Vanessa—you can tell that to Mr. Mainwaring for all I care—and I just can't imagine him killing himself, either. I'm sure you think I'm being naïve, but those are my feelings."

"I'm pretty sure what they're saying is his suicide will close the case."

"Not for me it won't. Nobody'll ever convince me he did either of those things. Oh, there's the doorbell. People have been sending flowers to the house. I wish they wouldn't. We'll just have to drag them all to the funeral home and the church. You'll have to excuse me now."

By the time I got back to the Skelly station, the onlookers and reporters had gone. Potter was standing next to a large metal box where his officers had been putting the evidence bags they'd been filling. Potter was talking to two of his men so I had time to scan the plastic bags. A quart of Hamm's beer, a half-finished sandwich of some kind, a pair of white socks with blood on the toe of one of them, a stadium blanket of deep blue with horizontal yellow stripes, a Greyhound bus schedule, a Swiss army knife, and a small black flashlight. There were many more items beneath these but I assumed Potter wouldn't be real happy if he saw me pawing through his evidence bags.

"Any sign of a note?" I asked Potter when he walked over to me.

"No, but there might be a good explanation for that, Sam. Maybe he just didn't have anything to write with."

"It's still strange."

"It's strange if you *want* it to be strange. Otherwise it's as simple as my explanation."

I nodded to where the ambulance had been. "The doc say anything unexpected?"

"Just that it looked like a suicide. He wanted to get Cameron on the table before he said it officially, but he said any other explanation was unlikely."

"All the evidence in the bags—will his sister get his belongings at some point?"

"At some point, yes. I imagine this thing'll end at the inquest. So it shouldn't take long. He killed himself."

From what Sarah Powers had told me, Neil Cameron had been a confused and angry man after he came back from Vietnam. The deaths he'd seen—and the lives he'd taken by mistake—had alienated him from not only others but himself as well. He'd come to rely on romance to redeem him, but when that had failed him, failed him because of his own obsessiveness and possessiveness, he'd started getting into even more trouble than he had previously. Then he'd met Vanessa and became even more desperate. Some of these facts would make their way into the inquest. They would convince everybody present that he'd been a prime candidate for suicide. He'd murdered his true love because she wouldn't have him and then in remorse taken his own life.

"I'd tell your friends at the commune it's probably time for them to move on, Sam. For everybody's sake, including theirs. I don't mind them as long as they don't break the law, but after all this, the city council's going to be on their ass for sure. They'll come up with some ordinance to run them out or to make their lives so miserable they'll want to leave anyway. Might as well get it over with now."

"I'll talk to them. But Richard Donovan has a temper and he isn't afraid of much. I doubt he'll listen. And I'm not sure they should be forced to move anyway. If Cameron did kill Vanessa Mainwaring, he acted alone. The others didn't have anything to do with it."

"Just trying to help. I want a nice, peaceful life. That's why I came out here. The hippies just seem to agitate a lot of people."

"And you know why that is, don't you?"

"The long hair?"

"All the sex. Everybody secretly wants to have as much sex as these kids have. But since they can't, they take it out on the hippies."

"You really believe that?"

I smiled. "Sometimes."

11

The first time I ever heard Judge Whitney call Richard Nixon "Dick" and Leonard Bernstein "Lenny," I was under the impression that she was making up her so-called relationships with these two gentlemen. But then "Dick" Nixon came and stayed with her at her manse and "Lenny" Bernstein started sending her both birthday and Christmas gifts. There was also the fact that she certainly had the opportunity to meet with them because she took at least four trips a year to New York City, where both men resided. She often said she could "breathe" in New York City, implying of course that she found our little city suffocating. She didn't try to hide her snobbery and maybe she didn't believe she was *being* snobbish. For a conservative Republican she was liberal when it came to civil rights and protecting the poor against the wealthy, and she became enraged whenever a group of local idiots tried to have this or that book banned from the public library.

She was a remarkable woman, given that she'd been married four times, no children, had managed to keep her looks even now into her sixties and, for good measure, had taught Barry Goldwater how to mambo. I'm not sure he *wanted* to learn how to mambo but the judge can be most persuasive at times. I know about the Goldwater tutorial because there's a black-and-white framed photo of it on the wall of her judicial chambers.

She's had her grief. Her deepest love was for her first husband, who was killed in the Pacific when our troops were getting slaughtered there early on. Her fourth husband died behind the wheel of a new Lincoln Continental while drunkenly escorting his drunken secretary to a motel where they were known as frequent guests. This didn't help her own reliance on alcohol. Finally, she checked herself into a rehabilitation clinic in Minnesota. She was now several years dry and a fervent attendee at AA meetings.

None of this had dulled her edge; nothing could. She was still imperious, and after all these years I wasn't sure that I wanted her any other way.

She stood in the sunlight arcing through the tall, mullioned window of the old courthouse. In her crisp peach-colored suit, her Gauloise cigarette streaming soft blue smoke from her fingers, she might have been a woman in one of those magazines only rich people read. Staring out at a polo match or the arrival of a head of state.

Without turning to look at me, she said: "My friends at the club very smugly told me that Cliffie has the Mainwaring murder solved and ready for the county attorney. It's even worse this morning. By the time I got to my chambers, four different people told me that they'd read the local rag, and apparently there's a quote from Cliffie—more or less in English—that he won't be 'outguessed' on this one. He also said that your friends, those dreadful 'hippies' as you call them, should be forced to leave town." Now she glared at me. "I don't want that illiterate fool outsmarting us on this one, McCain."

"He hasn't yet."

"Dummies have dumb luck. Maybe he's right for once."

She crossed the room with finishing school aplomb and set her quite fine bottom on the edge of her desk, Gauloise in one hand, her glass of Perrier in the other. "If this Cameron boy didn't kill her, why did he commit suicide?"

"I don't think it was suicide. And I'm hoping the doc agrees with me."

"The 'doc,'" she scoffed. "Somebody brought him as a guest to the club one night and he got three sheets to the wind and started talking about how stupid Republicans are. At the club, if you can imagine."

"I wish I could've been there."

"You'll never set foot in our club if I have anything to do with it. You'd be worse than he was. You'd probably start giving your Saul Alinsky speech."

Saul Alinsky was the Chicago professor famous for teaching groups that were powerless how to organize and become powerful. These groups were always the outsiders, ethnic and political ones looking for justice. "He's one of my heroes."

"What's wrong with William F. Buckley?"

"Too prissy and too smug."

"I'll mention that to Bill when I see him next month."

"I have several other things you could tell him, but you wouldn't want those words to come from your mouth."

A dramatic drag on the Gauloise: "So if he didn't kill her, who did?"

"Right now there are several possibilities. I wanted to ask you if you'd ever heard anything at your club about Eve Mainwaring."

She stretched her legs out, inspected them. Long and slender, perfectly turned. She had good wheels and knew it. "Personally, I like her. She's a bit standoffish, but that's only because when she first started coming there all the usual sex fiends started chasing her."

"Paul didn't object?"

"Paul wasn't around. God, that man travels more than LBJ. She usually came with one of the other club women."

"So you haven't heard anything about her?"

"That she sleeps around? Of course. I've heard it. But I don't believe it. I've talked to her a number of times. It turns out she loves Lenny's music."

"Ah."

"Don't think I don't know what's behind that 'Ah.' When I told her that Lenny was a friend of mine, she was fascinated and wanted to hear all about him. I consider that a sign of intelligence and sophistication."

"So you don't think any of the scuttlebutt about her is true?"

"I most certainly don't."

"I don't suppose she's a fan of Dick Nixon, too."

Another momentary indulgence on her cigarette: "I wouldn't be crude enough to ask, McCain. That's something people like you would do. She did say, however—and I had absolutely nothing to do with this—that she didn't think much of Hubert Humphrey. I'll let you make up your own mind on that."

"She's supporting George Wallace?"

She slipped off the desk. "I've had enough of you for today. Now get busy. I want to put a stop to all this nonsense about Cliffie having solved the case."

"If I pull it off will you invite me to your club?"

She couldn't help it. She smiled. "They'd eat you alive, McCain. And they wouldn't laugh at even one of your stupid jokes. Now get going."

The main floor of the courthouse held what was called a luncheonette. For employees of the courthouse it was perfect for quick breakfasts, quick lunches, and twenty-minute coffee breaks. Next to it stood a small stand run by a blind man named Phil Lynott. He'd gone to the Vinton School for the Blind back in the mid-'40s and had been running the stand ever since. He sold newspapers, cigarettes, cigars, and pipe tobacco. He was a rangy, balding man who wore dark glasses. He could tell you where every single item was. He could retrieve said item in seconds. Just about everybody liked him. One time a smart-ass, on a bet, tried to steal a newspaper. A big defense lawyer who'd played tackle for the U of Iowa got the culprit around the neck and damn near choked him to death. Phil had had no such trouble since.

"Hi, Phil. Did Cartwright finally convert you?"

Phil laughed. "You know he's on in the afternoon now, too." He nodded to his small black plastic radio.

"Oh, goody."

"Whatever else you can say about him, he's great entertainment."

"*. . . and so tonight in the park my flock will be presenting a one-act play called* Jesus Meets a Hippie. *This is something the entire family will want to see, especially if you've got boys or girls who think they might want to grow their hair long and take drugs and fornicate before marriage. As I said to my wife just the other night, when I think of all that fornicating I just can't get to sleep.*"

Phil's laughter rang off the sculpted halls of the courthouse. "'Don't bother me now, honey, I'm thinking of all that fornication.'" He was still laughing when I pushed through the heavy glass doors and stepped into the ninety-six-degree afternoon.

"She's in the bathroom."

Jamie was whispering. And pointing. As if I didn't know where the down-the-hall bathroom was.

"Who are we talking about?"

"Shh. Not so loud, Mr. C. She'll hear you."

I seated myself at my desk.

"She came in real mad and then she just sat there and started crying. I don't blame her. If my brother committed suicide I'd be half crazy, too. I feel sorry for her." She was still whispering.

Sarah Powers walked in then. "Jamie said it would be all right if we talked." She stood in front of my desk. The anger Jamie said she'd come in with had probably depleted her momentarily. "I want to thank you for getting me out of jail. I probably owe you some bail money."

"No bail, Sarah. I told them I wouldn't press charges against you for hitting me with that steel rod. And I convinced them you weren't being an uncooperative witness—that you didn't know any more than you were telling them."

"Well, I really appreciate it, Mr. McCain."

"I'm Sam. You're Sarah."

No smile, just a nod.

Jamie held up her bottle of Wite-Out, her lifeline to secretarial success. "I'm all out, Mr. C, I need to go get some more."

I knew she kept half a dozen emergency bottles in her desk. I was impressed that she'd devised such a clever way of excusing herself so I could talk with Sarah. Someday when I'm a little more successful I'll have an office with two rooms. I will stop people on the street to tell them about this and eventually two men in white will cart me off to the mental institution one town away while I'm babbling, "Two rooms, I tell ya! Two rooms!"

"Good idea, Jamie."

"You want me to bring you anything, Mr. C?"

"No, I'm fine. Thanks, though."

Jamie stood up, that wonderful dichotomy of *Teenage Babylon* body and Donna Reed face. In her pink summer dress—something Wendy and I had bought for her on her birthday—she was a sweet young mother. Married, unfortunately, to a little rat bastard who considered Iowa a surfing state. Have you ever seen a cow surf? Neither have I.

When we were alone, Sarah said, "He didn't kill himself."

"Why don't you sit down, Sarah? You look exhausted."

"I know my brother. He wouldn't kill himself."

"You said you were worried he'd kill himself when he got strung out on that one girl."

She was still standing up. "I shouldn't have said that. Deep down I didn't believe he would have. And I don't believe it now."

I pointed to the chair. She finally walked back to the most comfortable chair in the place, the one I'd bought when the largest law firm in the city redid their offices and sold off most of their old furniture.

"He didn't commit suicide and he didn't kill her."

"I believe he didn't kill her. I'm not as sure about him committing suicide, though for some reason I tend to agree with you. I think he was murdered."

"You mean that?" She looked younger then, still and always the tomboy, but there was a childlike frailty in the dark gaze now as if she'd finally found a true friend. I could abide her usual anger because I could understand it but it was pleasant to see her almost winsome.

"There's something I got from one of the girls at the commune. Emma Ewing. She said that just before dusk she saw Bobby Randall's Thunderbird parked down by the barn. He was talking to Donovan. She was in the house for maybe twenty minutes, and when she came out again his Thunderbird was still there but she didn't see him anywhere."

"He comes there a lot?"

The eyes got shrewd. "Nobody told you?"

"Told me what?"

"A lot of us think he's got a deal with Donovan."

"What kind of deal?"

"Donovan says that we should only buy drugs from Randall. He said that right after we moved in. He says Randall's the only one we know isn't a narc."

"So he gets a cut from Randall?"

"We can't prove it but that's what we think. And you know Donovan went after Vanessa before my brother did. He was way hung up on her. He didn't go crazy like Neil but he started trying to sleep with every chick in the commune. He even hit on me a couple of times. I mean, guys don't hit on me unless they're really hard up."

"You've got to stop that. I do all right with women and look at me."

"There's nothing wrong with you."

"Oh, no? I'm short and I'm not exactly handsome. It's attitude. I just pretend I'm this cool guy and sometimes it works. And that's what you've got to do."

"I'm scared of guys."

"Well, I'm scared of women."

"Really?"

"Absolutely. They're like this alien species. Just when you think you've figured them out a little bit they do something completely unexpected. And you're standing there looking like a fool."

She must have been restraining herself to a painful degree because suddenly she was sobbing, her face in her hands. I walked around the desk and stood in back of her chair. I put my hands gently on her shoulders and started muttering all the stupid things people mutter at times like these, a reminder of how difficult it is to really comfort anyone.

I reached over and snatched Jamie's Kleenex box from her desk. I handed it to Sarah. She plucked one free. It resembled a fluttering white bird in her fingers. She blew her nose but kept on sobbing.

When the phone rang, I took it on Jamie's desk. Paul Mainwaring didn't say hello. "I've sent you a check for a thousand dollars, Sam. That should be enough for your services."

"Way *too* much, actually."

"It's done. We have our answers. Now we can get on with our grieving. I appreciate your work on this, Sam."

"Shouldn't we wait for the autopsy?"

He wasn't angry; peeved was the word here. "Autopsy? We already have it. Vanessa was stabbed to death."

"I mean Neil Cameron's autopsy."

"What's that got to do with anything? Now I'm in a hurry here, Sam. As I said, I've sent you a check for a thousand dollars and I've thanked you for your work and I'm hanging up now."

"What if Neil didn't commit suicide?" I rushed my words, had to because he was about to put his phone down.

Peevishness was now anger. "He did commit suicide, Sam. That's obvious to everyone except you, apparently. I talked to Mike Potter. His opinion is that Cameron felt guilty about killing my daughter and that he knew he'd spend the rest of his life in prison so he killed himself. Even you should be able to understand that, Sam."

Yes, even you, Sam. Now quit picking bugs off yourself and begging for bananas and get off the damn phone!

"Potter hasn't seen the autopsy yet, either. Maybe he'll change his mind."

"Good-bye, Sam. I wanted this to be a pleasant little call because right now I'm losing my mind over my daughter's death and I need a lot of little pleasant moments. But thanks to you I'm all worked up again. Good-bye."

Sarah was dabbing her eyes with the Kleenex. The sobs had given way to frantic sighs. I got myself a cup of coffee and said, "Where're you planning to stay?"

"At the commune, why?"

"Everything be cool there for you?"

"Yeah, except for Richard. He's pissed because all this is likely to get the commune shut down. That's the only thing he talked about. He didn't say anything about Neil being dead. I think he still hated him because of Vanessa."

"But Vanessa ended up doing the same thing to Neil that she did to Donovan, right?"

"The same thing she did to all her boyfriends. They'd get close and then she'd dump them. But Richard couldn't see it that way. When he'd drink he'd talk about how he'd still be with her if it wasn't for Neil."

"So it doesn't bother you to go back there?"

"The people there are more my friends than Richard's. They're tired of him. This Emma I told you about?" A fleeting smile. "She calls him The Overlord."

Jamie was back with two sacks. One was from the office supply store, the other from the deli. She placed the former on her desk and the latter in Sarah's lap. "They were having a special on ham and cheese on rye so I thought I'd get you one. I'll get you some Pepsi from the machine down the hall."

"She sure is nice."

"She sure is, Sarah. And so are you. I'm going to find Bobby Randall and meanwhile you're invited to stay in this luxurious office of mine as long as you want to."

Jamie returned just as I spoke. "Don't worry, Mr. C. I'll take good care of her. I'll show her some of Laurie's baby pictures." She beamed down at Sarah. "Laurie's my baby." I was surprised she hadn't already told our guest all about her. People who've been in my office for more than three minutes usually know the whole story by heart.

12

I'd been to Bobby Randall's place only once. Two years ago a woman who worked in the courthouse asked me to tell him to stop seeing her sixteen-year-old daughter. He was, after all, in his early twenties. His age made him prosecutor bait but she didn't want to press charges because, she said, her daughter, who was very much taken with the handsome, arrogant Bobby, would never forgive her. The woman told me that she had nightmares of her daughter getting pregnant.

I'd seen Bobby around town. In his red Thunderbird he was hard to miss. His trail of heartbroken women provided tavern talk for other young men. Bobby was not beloved. In the words of the Everly Brothers, he was a bird dog. He seemed to take particular pride in sleeping with women who were affixed to boyfriends, fiancés, and husbands. He had the looks, all dark curly hair and features that were almost pretty, and swagger that would put my favorite draft dodger John Wayne to shame.

As I pulled into the alley where he had turned a three-car garage into his workshop, I heard the competing sounds of rock music and circular saw. I pulled off the gravel onto blanched grass crosscut with tire tracks. This was the visitor parking area.

The doors were wide open, allowing in heat and flying kamikaze bugs. The setup was impressive. Lighting was provided by overhead fluorescents. The walls were covered with shelving and pegboard that contained hammers, pliers, extra saw blades, screwdrivers, and so many other things that I gave up looking. He was cutting two-by-fours on a workbench big enough to play Ping-Pong on. He stood in a T-shirt and jeans on a floor of wood that he'd covered with a linoleumlike surface. Everything was bright and new, as if it would be used for a photo in a trade magazine. The one element that enhanced even the splendor of the workshop was the splendor of the blonde in the very tight Levi's cutoffs and braless pink T-shirt who sat perched on a stool in the corner. She held a long cigarette in one hand and a magazine in the other. Neither she nor Randall looked up when I entered because neither could hear me above the whine of the saw. The smell of freshly sawn wood took me back to the days when I was little and watched my father make wonderful things in his own tiny workshop.

When he'd shaved as much as he'd wanted to off the two-by-four he reached down for another board and that's when he saw me. His first reaction was anger. He changed it quickly to a smug smile. "I could have you arrested for trespassing."

"Who is he, Bobby?" She was the mythic mountain girl in all of Charles Williams's Gold Medal novels, pure animal sex and ravishing insolence. The voice didn't work with the body—cigarettes and booze and, likely, drugs.

"He's a nobody who thinks he's somebody because he works for Judge Whitney."

"That bitch. She put my brother in county for six months."

"You don't have any friends here, McCain." He lifted his saw and jabbed it in my direction. "So if I was you, I'd leave right now."

"You could take him one-handed, Bobby. He don't even come up to your shoulders."

Bobby nodded to the blonde who was, for all her looks, a pretty nasty lady.

"She's got two brothers, McCain. She grew up watching them beat the hell out of each other. She knows about fighting. If she says I can whip your ass, take her word for it."

"How much dope were you selling Vanessa Mainwaring?"

That got us past the tough-guy talk.

The dark eyes narrowed in fear.

"A murder like that, the police are going to start looking into her background for the county attorney. The drugs'll come up and your name is going to be in the papers and on TV." It was bullshit but he was too dumb to know that. "You're going to find yourself up against some heavy-duty charges. Paul Mainwaring's going to see that you get put away for a long time."

The blonde started to say something but stopped herself. She had a scorching glare. I could almost feel my skin shrivel.

"The kind of business you're in, Bobby, you'll be lucky to get out in fifteen years."

"You bastard. You've been waitin' to nail me, haven't you, McCain?"

"You're wasting my time, Randall. I want to know how much dope she was buying and what kind."

"And then you run to the cops."

"Or that bitch of a judge." Blondie.

"Your Thunderbird was parked outside the barn where Vanessa's body was found."

He finally put the saw down. He made a show of flexing his bicep as he did so. Even in panic he had to peacock it. "So what?"

"Your car was there during the time the coroner said she was killed. So where were you?"

"You don't have to tell him nothing, Bobby. It's two against one. All we gotta say is he made alla this up."

"I just walked around the commune the way I usually do, McCain. I like the fresh air out there."

God had provided Randall with enviable skills—enviable to me anyway—as a carpenter and handyman. His law degree was apparently still in the mail.

"Mike Potter has checked all the footprints in the barn. He's accounted for all of them except two. I haven't mentioned you to him yet. But how would you like it if I went straight from here to a phone and told him to check out all your shoes?"

Even Blondie gulped when I said this. For just a second not even her cunning could disguise her apprehension. I wasn't sure what they were hiding from me but obviously I'd made both of them nervous.

"Let's go back to the dope. How much and what kind?"

"This is really bullshit, man. Like I said, I could charge you with trespassing."

"Yeah, you could. And I could always call Mike Potter. How about if we swap, Randall? You tell me about the drugs and I won't tell Potter anything if I believe you're telling me the truth."

"Don't tell him anything, Bobby. That bitch judge of his'll just put you in prison the same way she did Ronnie."

How could anybody as ravishing—and she was—as Blondie be such a bitch? And not exactly a bright one at that.

"I wouldn't listen to her, Bobby. She wouldn't be able to help you when Potter and the county attorney started snooping around. I can help you if you help me now."

"You back off, Dodie. I gotta be careful here."

Dodie? I had nothing against the name but somehow she wasn't a "Dodie." Dodies are cute and pert in my mind; this Dodie was a long-legged female swashbuckler who used sex and her belligerent mouth to get her way. Dodie?

Dodie slid off the stool and came up to stand next to Randall. She stood hip-cocked and spectacular. Just as long as she didn't open her mouth. "He's conning you."

"Maybe so, but I want to hear him out at least. Why don't you go in and see about supper?"

"I want to stay here."

At this rate ol' Bobby was soon going to get kicked out of the He-Man Club. You know, the guys who don't take crap off anybody, especially women. Dodie-with-the-unlikely-name was clearly in charge here.

"All right, but keep quiet."

"I'll keep quiet as long as you don't say anything stupid to this asshole."

When I thought about it, I could almost feel sorry for Randall.

"How long were you selling her drugs?"

He glanced at Dodie as if seeking her permission to talk. To me he said, "Six, seven months."

"How often?"

"She was one of my best customers. Every seven or eight days or so."

"You ever think maybe he's wired and you're talking yourself into hard time?"

"I'm not wired, Randall. And you're doing the right thing. What kind of drugs did she buy?"

This time he didn't look for permission. "Across the board. At least of the kind I sell. Pot, speed, coke, acid. Once in a while I get weird shit like peyote or something. She liked acid. She loved tripping. The kids at the commune, all they ever want is pot and acid."

"You get to know her?"

Bobby Randall, cool cat and heartbreaker, blushed, which wasn't doing much for his image. The blooded cheeks told me that she had likely seduced him the way she'd likely seduced a lot of young men. He had to clear his throat to speak. "Talked to her a little bit."

"That better be all you did."

"Dodie, I already told ya nothin' happened."

"I seen her. And I seen the way you looked at her."

"Yeah, well, nothin' happened."

"Why was your car there so long last night?"

This time he didn't blush. He lowered his head and stared at the ground for half a minute. Then he looked up and said, "Remember, it's two to one. Your word against ours."

"You can relax, Randall. I think you're a scumbag but right now I could give a rat's ass about your drug deals. I want to find out who murdered Vanessa and Neil Cameron. So what were you doing there so long?"

"Don't tell him anything more, Bobby. He's got enough to put you away already."

"None of this goes to the cops, right?"

"They'll nail your ass soon enough. They don't need any help from me. I won't repeat anything we talked about here today."

He pawed at his face, the same thing I'd been doing to mine. Between the heat Dodie was exuding and the temperature, Randall's garage was one steamy place.

"Me'n Richard—Richard Donovan?—we got a deal. I give him a cut and he tells all his people to buy strictly from me. I've been worried about cops so Richard agreed to let me put my stash in the barn. I was unloading then covering it up. And I didn't see any dead Vanessa."

"How did Richard act when you got there?"

He was in need of permission again. A quick glance to Dodie then back to me: "Kinda nervous. That doesn't mean anything. All the drugs I was hiding, I was nervous, too."

"Did you hide them in the front of the barn or in the back?"

"Front. Richard had dug this deep hole, then I had to dig another one. Then we went to my trunk and started loading everything into these army ammunition boxes. You know, metal, and they'd lock real tight. Then we pushed an old refrigerator over the holes we dug."

Sounded feasible but this was Bobby Randall. I trusted him slightly less than I did Dick Nixon.

"I guess that'll be it for now, Randall."

"You happy, you dumb bastard? You just talked your way into prison."

"She's a sweetie, Randall. Make sure you keep her."

He sighed and shrugged. I gazed into the blazing eyes of Dodie Dear, then I did some shrugging myself and started walking toward the alley. I got my last glimpse of his site. My father would have been overwhelmed by the entire arrangement.

I had just about reached the door when I heard Randall shout: "McCain, duck!"

I pitched myself leftward just in time to see a hammer flying toward the point where my head had been a moment ago.

"You better watch out for Ronnie and Donnie," she screamed. "They'll make you sorry you were ever born!"

And in this moment of Mountain Beauties slinging hammers at me, Randall shouted out the most preposterous thing of all. "Take a flier with you, McCain. In case you know somebody who needs some carpentry work."

Right next to the door was a straight-back chair with fliers piled on it. And damned if I didn't pick one up.

13

I hadn't asked Bobby Randall about Eve Mainwaring. I was lucky he'd told me as much as he had, especially with Mountain Girl there. I doubted he'd talk about Paul's wife anyway. If his story was true about working with Donovan to off-load all his dope, then he had a good excuse—as opposed to an alibi—to be out at the commune. And to spend so much time near the barn. Eve Mainwaring was another matter. I wondered—and he had to be wondering, too—what his carpentry customers would think of him if they knew that he was sleeping with the wife of a man who'd hired him as a handyman.

With his flier on my passenger seat I drove the twenty-eight miles to the Sleepy Time Motel, the just-far-enough-away concrete bunker where you went when you were too scared to try it close to home. Given all the sneaking around and close calls, adultery should be an Olympic sport.

On a summer afternoon when the sun bragged on how mean it could be, I wanted my old Ford ragtop back. And I wanted my father to be alive. And I wanted my mother to make a life for herself, not turn into one of the old ladies who spend most of their free time in church, arthritic hands entwined with rosaries, and memories their only comfort. And I wanted to convince Wendy to marry me, to take the chance at least a part of her knew was worth it.

The radio was still filled with responses to the police riot at the Democratic convention. Mayor Daley was denying he'd made any anti-Semitic remarks, and the police commissioner just couldn't find a single thing his officers had done wrong. It was all the fault of the "anarchists." Somebody from the police union gave an even stronger defense of the cops. He talked about all the danger they'd faced that night, even though they were the ones with the clubs and guns and punitive rage. Never a mention about how we were feeding an entire generation into the bloody maw of an unnecessary war and how the president and the Pentagon lied every single day to the American people—the president worried about his place in history and the Pentagon not wanting to stop the flow of money to the great war machine Eisenhower had warned about as he left office. The kids weren't in the streets to have a good time—though some were, I suppose. They were there to protest their lives being wasted on the lies of old men.

The Sleepy Time didn't resemble a hot-sheet motel. It sat on a hill overlooking a leg of river and a picnic area on the bank. The colors of the office and the room exteriors were two shades of brown—the paint fresh—and the macadam was new. To the left of the office was a swimming pool where a lone young man practiced diving. It was too hot for tanning or sitting around to talk. The middle-aged woman behind the desk was California, tanned, freckled, pretty, her blonde hair streaked even blonder by the sun. Her energy and good nature were just short of aggressive. In her yellow blouse and long silver earrings she was well worth my attention.

"Let me guess." Alluring smile. "You don't want a room."

"You're a fortune teller."

"No. After twenty years in this business I'm just observant. The way you looked around on the drive and the way you came through the door over there told me that you weren't going to be a guest."

"Any guess why I'm here?"

"A cop or something like that. Which I think is cool. Breaks up the monotony. We're full up and everybody's behaving so I don't have much to do. My husband's in the hospital with back problems and my son's getting ready for his next swim meet so I'm all alone in here with my soap operas." Her teeth were luminous against her tanned face. "If you're not a cop you're a private investigator, and if you're a private investigator somebody hired you to find out about somebody cheating."

"You're doing most of my work for me."

"We run a respectable place. And a nice place. But we're not above letting our rooms to people who aren't married to each other. We make them pay full price for the privilege. That way we keep a reasonably suitable clientele. Not always, but most of the time."

"You ever had any trouble?"

"Oh, sure. But fortunately Frank, my husband, he was a marine in Korea and he's kept in good shape except for his back. He's had to handle some angry husbands who've followed their wives here. And once there was a homosexual man whose boyfriend followed him here with a gun. Frank handles everything himself. We don't want any unnecessary bad publicity. I wish he was here now. My husband's the funniest guy I've ever known. It's never boring when he's around."

I slid Bobby Randall's flier across the desk. She smiled when she saw it. "Oh, yes, Johnny. So his real name's Bobby?"

"Uh-huh. He's been here then?"

"I'd have to say no comment. The way politicians do."

"What if I told you a man's future depended on what I'm doing. An innocent man." It wasn't true but it sure sounded good.

That sun-blessed face wrinkled in suspicion. "Who exactly are you?"

I showed her my ID. "A young woman was murdered in Black River Falls last night."

"Yeah. That was sure a bummer. But they've already said that the guy who killed her committed suicide."

Time for another somewhat untrue statement. "They're saying that to trap the real killer. Or anyway the man they *think* is the real killer. He's a client of mine. I'm trying to help him. I don't want to see him railroaded into prison. I have a feeling you can help me and nobody ever needs to know. Not even your husband."

That sand and ocean smile. "Now you sound like some of our customers."

"So how about it?"

"Well—" She dragged out the word. "If you promise me you'll never use my name."

I used the three-finger pledge. "Scout's honor."

A nice surfy laugh. "Well, if you put it that way."

"So how about Bobby? He's been here?"

"Many times." A laugh. "Frank has a short list of men he calls 'living legends' and Johnny's one of them. I like Johnny better than Bobby if you don't mind. I had a bad experience with a Bobby when I was in high school. I hate people named Bobby."

"Sounds reasonable."

She laughed again. "Sarcasm. You and my husband would get along. He's always saying things like that. I know it's irrational but that's the way I am."

"So about Johnny-Bobby."

"Well, actually, our son Steve probably knows more than we do. He works nights and that's when Johnny usually shows up. He isn't exactly secretive, though. I mean the red Thunderbird."

"But you've signed him in yourself?"

"Oh, sure. Several times."

"I'm going to describe a woman. If you've dealt with her I'd appreciate you telling me."

"Wait a minute here. This is starting to make me very nervous." The good nature vanished. A surprising harshness was in the voice and blue eyes. "This is our livelihood we're talking about here."

"I already promised you there won't be any trouble."

"Uh-huh, that's another thing you have in common with my Frank. You're both bullshit artists."

"So you're just going to stop here?"

She made a fist of a tanned, freckled hand. The knuckles were bone-white. "Goddammit, I shouldn't have told you anything."

"Well, you've told me this much. How about just a few more questions?"

"Shit. How do I get into things like this anyway?" Then: "All right, goddammit, go ahead."

I described Eve Mainwaring in as much detail as I could remember.

"You mean Andrea Cummings."

"Good old Andrea. So you've dealt with her?"

"Just twice. Both times when she was with Johnny. Johnny should learn not to park so close to the office. I can see in the car windows. Andrea was sitting there waiting for him to come back with the room key. Listen, let me get Steve. I'll be right back."

She moved from behind the desk to the front door, quick and lithe, very healthy in the way of the middle-aged people you saw in advertisements shot on the beach. While she was gone I stared through the open door behind the desk. A black-and-white set played a soap opera. This one had everything. A man whose face was entirely wrapped in gauze, a weeping middle-aged beauty, and a sullen-looking hippie punk of sixteen or so. The beauty was shrieking at the punk that he had no respect for his parents. The punk just got more sullen and then pointed to the masked man. Then he shouted that she was his mom but the masked man wasn't his father, that his real father was a man she'd had a fling with. The masked man slapped his hand to his heart. A monitor broke into ominous beeping. Take my word for it, the whole thing was one hell of a mess.

Steve had dragged on a red shirt and a pair of jeans. He was still scrubbing his hair with a towel. He had the same freckled, exuberant air of his mother but not her good looks. He handled me with the skill of a politician. "Nice to meet you, Mr. McCain. Mom says you wanted to ask me about Johnny and Andrea Cummings."

"I also said your dad's not to know anything about this conversation."

Steve grinned. "You don't have to worry about that. I'd be in trouble with Dad for talking to Mr. McCain, too."

"The only reason I'm doing this is because McCain here says an innocent man could be accused of a murder."

"Just like a movie, huh, Mom."

Mom stood next to him, her proud smile possessive of her boy. "That's right, honey. Now go ahead and answer the man's questions."

"Your mother said you've checked Johnny and Andrea Cummings in a few times."

"More than a few times, in fact, Mr. McCain. Sometimes they're with each other and sometimes they're with other people."

"That's what I'd like to talk about. Andrea Cummings—can you describe some of the other men she's been with?"

"Well, over the past year I'd say there're probably five or six at least."

"He's got a good memory. He's a straight-A student."

"Oh, Mom."

"Well, it's true."

"She doesn't think that's embarrassing, Mr. McCain. Anyway, I can probably describe three of them because they've been with her a number of times. A couple of them were only out here once with her. Or maybe twice, but no more than that."

I took out my nickel notebook and wrote down his descriptions. Andrea-Eve was apparently no snob. One of the men was a handsome professorial sort, one was a tennis instructor from a nearby racquet club, and one, the boy felt sure, was some kind of criminal. "He just had that look."

"He likes crime shows on TV."

"Could you be a little more specific about the criminal?"

"Well, for one thing, he always wore short-sleeved shirts even in the winter and he had tattoos on both arms. A panther on his right and a tiger on his left. He had real hairy arms. I guess I associate tattoos with criminals."

"Was there ever any trouble?"

"I guess I don't know what you mean."

"Did other guests complain about noise—fights or screaming, anything like that?"

"Oh, no. They were always nice. Even the guy with the tattoos. If anybody was going to cause trouble, it was him."

"Did they ever ask you for any special favors? Like maybe getting them a bottle of liquor or something?"

"I'm not old enough to buy liquor."

The kid was a Boy Scout. He'd never heard of motel desk clerks who provided customers with bottles or babes. The Sleepy Time was a downright boring place.

"Well, the guy with the tattoos asked me if we had one of those machines where you could buy those things but I said no. It was kind of embarrassing."

I assumed he meant rubbers.

"When was the last time Andrea Cummings was here?"

"Just last week. With Johnny again. They didn't stay as long as usual and Johnny was in a hurry when he dropped off the key. He usually likes to talk."

"About what?"

"He usually talks about the Hawkeye football or basketball team, whichever one is in season. But this time he just tossed the keys on the counter and walked right out."

"I told you he had a good memory. Frank's the same way."

I closed my notebook and shoved it into my back pocket. I had already concocted a theory in the way of good private investigators everywhere. It was Eve-Andrea who killed Vanessa. Van learned about Eve cheating on Paul and threatened to tell her father if Eve didn't divorce Paul and leave. And since Van had confided in Neil Cameron about Eve, Cameron had to die, too, which Eve-Andrea accomplished by having one of her numerous lovers, probably the one with the tattoos, help her. See how simple things are when you have no idea what you're talking about?

"I appreciate your help very much, both of you."

As I started for the door, the woman called, "I sure hope the cops don't start hassling your man. I'm used to L.A. cops. They're the worst."

14

I was at Wendy's in time for supper. For once. Since it was so hot even with the air conditioning on, we had one of those cold suppers that are often tastier than the hot ones. Slices of fresh watermelon and cantaloupe, a spinach salad with ranch dressing, and slices of wheat bread that Wendy had made during the day. She said it was a beer night rather than a wine night. I didn't disagree. I drank a can and a half of Schlitz but was too full to finish the rest.

Wendy had allowed me to bring my cats from my apartment, the ones I was allegedly still keeping for the old friend of mine who'd gone to L.A. to become an actress. The last I'd heard she was married to a cop and living in the valley with their first child. Tasha, Crystal, and Tess were thus mine. I told Wendy that they were my dowry.

The three of them sat on the far end of the dining room table watching us eat.

"Do you ever wonder what they're thinking about, Sam?"

"I know what they're thinking about."

"Oh, right."

"They're thinking how can a woman this gorgeous put up with a loser like McCain."

"That's funny. That's what *I* thought they were thinking, too. They're very perceptive."

She sipped her beer. I liked to watch her wrists. They were delicately wrought and charming all by themselves. Of course it would be difficult to date just a pair of wrists. People would talk. "God, you'd think Eve would be more careful."

"Maybe she's a nympho," I said.

"Nymphos are only in all those paperbacks you read."

"Well then she's super horny."

"Or something. Maybe she's going through the same thing *I* was when I was running around. I'm sure people called *me* a 'nympho,' too. But I wasn't married. I was only hurting myself and my mother and sister. She's hurting a husband."

"I wonder what kind of agreement they have about money. In case of a divorce."

"She wouldn't be in a position to say much if he just cut her off."

"Not unless there was some kind of cruelty going on, physical cruelty, and even then the judge would ask her why she hadn't reported it. He'd also tell her that running around was no way to deal with marital problems."

All three cats looked toward the front of the house when the doorbell rang. Tasha yawned, indicating that she thought whoever had come calling was bound to be boring.

"I'll get it." She was up before I could offer to do it, giving me a prolonged gape at her smooth tanned legs in white shorts. The red cotton blouse accented her small perfect breasts. She was still talking. "You don't really think Eve killed Vanessa and the Cameron boy, do you?"

"It's worth considering, anyway."

When she got the door open, she said, "It's Kenny." She did her best to pack excitement into those two words. She still wished Kenny didn't write soft-core sex books for a living, but he'd won her over with his wife Sue and his daughter Melissa. I think she liked Kenny without quite approving of him.

"Hi, Wendy. I hope I'm not interrupting dinner."

"No, not at all. We're finished. Come on in and have some coffee." An afterthought: "Or a beer."

Kenny had been here many times to see me. He was careful with his cigarettes (Kenny was an ash-flicker, and ashes on couches and chairs can mightily displease the hostess) as well as his language. "Coffee's fine," he said as he seated himself at the table. He was, in his words, "duded up." Starched white short-sleeved shirt with a red-and-black striped tie. And it wasn't a clip-on. I wondered where he'd been or where he was going. As Wendy was pouring him a cup of coffee, he said, "How much would you charge me to sue somebody for slander?"

"Are you serious?"

"Very serious."

"Who's slandering you?"

"From what I've been told, Reverend Cartwright is going to do it tonight in that moronic hippie play he's giving in the park."

"Who told you he was going to do it?"

"You know Mrs. Windmere from his church?"

Wendy laughed. "That old gossip? She used to help my mother clean house. We had to let her go because she made up these stories about what a sinful family we were. She even got Cartwright to show up one night and tell my dad that he was going to save our souls. My mother thought it was hilarious. My dad was so mad he grabbed Cartwright and threw him out the open doorway. I wouldn't believe a word she said, Kenny."

"How did you get hooked up with the Windmere woman, anyway?"

"I was having a cherry Coke at the Rexall fountain and she came up and told me that somebody was finally going to stand up to me.

It took me a few minutes but then I remembered who she was. She was the old bag who chased me down the street one day. She kept screaming, 'Repent! Repent!' So here she was again. Of course I didn't have any idea of what she was raving on about. I was so embarrassed I could barely hear her anyway. You know how I hate scenes. All these people were standing around watching and listening now and then she said it: 'Reverend Cartwright has written you into his play. Finally, a man of God is going to treat you the way you deserve to be treated.' Then she looked around at everybody and pointed to me and said, 'This man is a pronographer.'"

"'Pronographer'?" I said.

Wendy giggled. "Oh, God, that's right, Kenny. I forgot. Mrs. Windmere is always mispronouncing words."

"So I want to sue him."

"How about we wait until you see the show?"

He sat back in his chair, calm for the moment. "That's what I wanted to ask you two about. I really don't want to go alone. I even dressed up for the occasion so nobody could call me a hippie."

"Won't Sue go with you?"

"She would have, Wendy, but she doesn't want to take Melissa out into all that heat. You know, with the bugs and all."

"I'm sort of a baby myself, Kenny. I kind of like it here, you know, with the air conditioning and all. And the TV set and the indoor plumbing and the nice cold beer. But I'm sure your friend and mine Sam would love to go with you."

"Really? Damn it, Kenny, I don't want to go see that stupid show. It'll probably be crowded."

"You really think it'll be crowded?" Wendy said.

"Sure. All of Cartwright's people'll show up and then all the hecklers. Cliffie'll have a couple cops there to keep the hecklers in line but they have a way of getting heard no matter what."

"I don't want to remind you of all the information I get for you, McCain. And I do it free gratis."

"Oh, that's right. You'd never want to remind me of that, would you?"

"Maybe it'll be fun."

"Well, if you think it might be fun, Wendy, why don't you go?"

"I miss out on all kinds of fun, Sam, and you know it. And at my advanced age it doesn't bother me."

"If he slanders me, McCain, we can sue him for millions."

"He doesn't have millions, Kenny."

"Well, maybe we can at least get him off the air."

Knowing I was going to go, I said, "That's the first real incentive you've given me all night, Kenny. Let me change my clothes."

As I was closing the bathroom door, I heard Wendy say, "I knew you could talk him into it, Kenny. He's a pushover. But that's why we love him."

There's a librarian named Trixie Easley who sets up displays of old photographs from time to time. Generally these deal with our town from the 1870s to today. The pictures of the stage next to the bandstand in the city park are especially helpful for time traveling because in the various shots you see the town, the people, the clothes, the transportation, and the plays themselves as they fade era into era.

For the dapper, for instance, homburgs gave way to straw boaters and eventually to felt hats such as fedoras. For women, hats ranged from bonnets to fancy straw to cloche to pillbox and variations thereof. The vehicles were equally interesting—from wagons to surreys to comic-looking early automobiles to family Fords to flivvers to the sedans of today. When I was young I'd look at the people in these photographs and think how easy life had been for them psychologically. There was always so much flag-waving and spirited talk about hardy souls and all that they seemed like a different species. But as I got older I knew that these mythic generations were just that, mythic. They trod through this vale of tears just like every generation. To confirm that truth all you have to do is read the newspapers and police reports of that time. I took ironic comfort in that fact; what did I have to bitch about when every generation had faced the same travails and terrors we have? And they didn't even have Walter Cronkite.

Downtown was bright and crowded. Cliffie had put several extra cops on the street. We had to park three blocks away. The air was turgid and hot. The sidewalks were full of people hurrying. Even from this distance we could hear recordings of Reverend Cartwright singing. He hawked his records along with his diet tip books and his collected sermons, you know, just the way Jesus did.

Wolf packs of teenagers filled the streets with their low-slung cherry bomb mufflers competing with the tinny voice of the good reverend. As we reached the edge of the tiny park I saw that my prediction had been accurate. Gathered close to the stage were the faithful, probably a couple hundred of them. This was strictly BYOS, bring your own seating. They sat on lawn chairs, blankets, and even a few air cushions. Most of them had come family-size, wee ones as well as kids as old as sixteen or so. I had to wonder how many of the older ones had had to be dragged here tonight. Or maybe that was just my cynicism. Many of them could be just as sincerely devout as their parents.

Behind them were the smart-asses. You could identify them easily by their cigarettes, long hair, and smirks. Cops walked up and down in front of them, like army sergeants assessing their men. Cliffie would have given them strict orders to take no shit whatsoever. He was probably right in doing so. Abhorrent as Cartwright was—not to mention stone insane—he and his followers had the right to watch the play in peace. Of course when I was a teenager I might well have been one of the smirkers out tonight.

While the smirkers weren't officially hippies—they got into too many fights to be all peace-and-love-brother about life—a number of them affected hippie styles. Bell-bottoms, vests, tie-dyed T-shirts, and peasant blouses and long full skirts for the girls. A number of girls had come braless and that was all to the good. A new crew of them arrived in an elderly van painted with flowers and a peace sign.

The stage was long and flat, buttressed by folding metal props beneath. Behind it were heavy wine-colored curtains held up by thick steel rods. You could set up and take down the stage easily. Over the years it has been used by some actual celebrities. Kate Smith sang here pushing war bonds during WWII. Johnny Ray appeared here pushing for the polio drive, then the scourge of young and old alike. And most recently a local kid named Ryan Boggs had brought his guitar and a three-piece combo here to sing his one-and-only hit song that had won him a spot on *American Bandstand* and *The Lloyd Thaxton Show*. He was riding a little too high one night in the Quad Cities when some loudmouth picked a fight with him. The guy swung on Boggs and Boggs hit him back. In falling down, the loudmouth hit his head on the metal edge of the footing underneath the bar and died. Boggs's record company decided that Johnny was not a "decent representative of American youth" and canned his ass. He now plays beer parlors.

The first person to appear on stage was a teenager dressed up in a long-haired wig and a tie-dyed T-shirt covered in so many love beads he would probably suffer a neck injury from trying to support them. He wore jeans torn at the knees. He was barefoot. He came mid-stage. There were enough standing microphones to pick up just about every word. Music came up, sounding like Lawrence Welk playing something by The Doors.

The one thing the faux hippie was good at was portraying insolence. I wanted to slap the bastard across the fake beard and mustache. I knew tonight was going to be nothing but stereotypes, but nobody needed to make this town any more unfriendly to hippies. Even though the majority of citizens believe in live and let live, the aginners always spoke louder.

Subtle he wasn't. He pulled from his front pocket a twisted runt of a cigarette. "Tune in, turn on, and drop out. Those are my words to live by. Excuse me a second." He lit the joint, inhaled deeply, held it, then exploded smoke from his lungs. "If everybody smoked a little dope, this'd be a cool, cool world."

The smirkers were nudging each other and grinning. The cops were giving them dungeon looks.

"I bet if Jesus was alive today he'd be smoking joints right along with the rest of us."

Now it was the turn of the followers to react. Some booed; others poked each other and shook their heads.

"And he'd be into a lot of things the squares don't understand. Like how everything should be free and how people like me should run the government and how this whole war thing is a complete lie. He'd be on our side."

More subtlety. The sound effects of lightning and thunder, the music quick-fading underneath. The whole stage shook. And then from behind the drapes a new character appeared, the Lord Jesus Christ himself. He was tall, he was bearded, he wore the flowing white robe of all the traditional paintings. The one difference was the face. Where Christ was usually portrayed in a sentimental, almost sweet way, this Christ looked like he'd kill your mother for fifty cents. The broken nose, the long scar on the left cheek, the big fists dangling from the arms.

And then he spoke. He had the voice you'd expect from that face—rough, deep, threatening. He walked right up to the hippie and slammed his hand into the kid's chest, shoving him back a few feet. The hippie almost went down. "You've got some of your hippie friends here. Bring them out. I want them to hear this, too." He snapped his fingers.

While we waited the half minute for four other hippies—two girls, two boys—to appear, Kenny leaned in and said, "You know that bumper sticker: 'Jesus is coming and boy is he pissed'?"

My laugh was loud enough to attract attention, including that of the cops. Kenny was right. I had been raised to believe that Jesus Christ had been an understanding and forgiving man who helped the sick and the poor and the troubled. That was the Jesus I loved— whether he was merely man or son of God didn't matter much to me—and this cartoon travesty was perverse even for Reverend Cartwright.

All four of the new hippies wore wigs, meaning that they were the children of church members where long hair, among many, many other things, was forbidden.

"Now get this and get this straight. I'm going to tell you how to live the right way and unless you want to go straight to hell when you die, you better listen to me. You got that?"

The hippies all pretended to be terrified. They looked like bad actors in old silent films, hands over their faces as if trying to repel an attack, one of them falling to her knees and folding her hands in eager prayer. And they all chorused, "Yes, Jesus! Yes!"

"You know how in the Western movies there are towns that need to be tamed? Well, that's what you're going to do right here. And you're going to start right now. No more drugs, no more sex before marriage, no more pornography reading *or* writing and no more rock and roll."

They faked confusion, standing there in their bell-bottoms and tie-dyes and wigs, looking at each other in theatrical bafflement. Finally, the girl rose from her knees and said, "But how can we do this, Lord?"

There was a long pause filled with babies crying. A few of the smirkers were lighting joints.

"I am going to send one of my most loyal servants to the mountain the way it was done in Biblical times. There he will commune with me so that when he returns he will share my message with you. And from that message you will learn how to rid your town of the filth that stalks your streets."

The sound effects were better than I would have thought. Crackling lightning, deafening thunder.

And while it was startling the ears, the good Reverend Cartwright strode onto the stage wearing colorful biblical robes and carrying a staff. This was a very different get-up from the recent time when he'd set himself on fire trying to burn Beatles records. You had to admire him for trying again. Of course, being Cartwright, he stumbled as he moved to center stage.

He threw his hands wide the way he did when he healed people. His staff flew off stage right. And somewhere the kid with the tape recorder hit the thunder and lightning sound again.

"You heard the Lord. I will go to Pearson's Peak, where I will wait until he contacts me with his word of how to bring this entire town to his ways. And I will broadcast my daily shows from there with a live remote so you will not have to fear for my well-being."

The smirkers were already laughing and shouting. "Pearson's Peak ain't a mountain!"

In case you allowed yourself to be misled by the biblical use of the word "mountain," just as there is no ocean or surf in Iowa, there are no mountains. Pearson's Peak is a tall spot of red clay above the river road. It is approximately a thirty-foot drop to the pavement below. Many years ago, back when even the most elegant among us still used outhouses, somebody sarcastically named it after Pike's Peak.

This was typical Cartwright, the whole thing. His followers genuinely wanted to run the hippies out of town, and no doubt Cartwright found them irritating. But this ham play and the word from the Lord was all to promote his radio show. I'm pretty sure Jesus never used a live remote, but then Jesus didn't have Cartwright's skill with self-promotion. Or confidence games if you prefer.

You see, Jesus ordered Cartwright to the mountain every year about this time. Cartwright did his communing inside a comfortable little trailer, while all around him were booths offering religious pamphlets he bought in bulk at two cents each and charged $2.50 for. Then there were his self-published books, record albums, children's books, and Jesus sweaters, caps, and jackets. His church ladies sold burgers and hot dogs and pop at jacked-up prices. And every time he emerged from his trailer to speak to the two or three hundred people who'd gathered there, a plate was passed around. The shakedowns never ended.

He kept talking, or tried to. The smirkers kept shouting insults and laughing at him. Not even the cops walking among them could shut them up. Cartwright's flock turned on the smirkers and started chanting their own cleaned-up insults right back. Cartwright the mountaineer was drowned out completely.

And then finally, it broke. Whether the smirkers rushed the followers or the followers rushed the smirkers, it was hard to say, but somebody threw a punch at somebody and about a dozen bodies were entangled in pushing, shoving, and throwing a few fists.

The cops rushed to form a broken line between the two groups. They shouted, too—for both groups to shut the hell up.

For the past few minutes I'd sensed somebody staring at me, but in all the shouting I hadn't looked around. Now that I started scanning the people behind me, I didn't see anybody taking any particular interest in me. These were the true onlookers. They'd come to the crash site just to check it out. They weren't followers and they weren't smirkers. I suspected that most of them in this blistering, sweaty night were here for the yuks. This might well be more interesting than anything on at the drive-in. (I'd checked and it was.) I started to look back at the groups who were bringing the cops to understandable anger. But then peripherally I caught somebody waving. He'd quit waving by the time I'd started looking again. I was about to give up when I saw him lean from behind a tree and wave again.

Tommy Delaney, high school football player and tortured soul of his parents' many deadly battles, walked in my direction. I thought maybe he'd seen somebody behind me he wanted to talk to, but then there he was putting out his hand.

As we shook he said, "I'm sorry I was such a jerk to you before, Mr. McCain. I ran into Sarah this afternoon and she told me you were a good guy and that I should apologize."

"I didn't know you and Sarah knew each other."

"Yeah. My uncle owns the used-book store over on Main and Chandler. I used to work there sometimes. She was always coming in. She's a big reader." He had a shy smile. "We didn't get along at first. You know, she can come on pretty strong with the hippie stuff. But eventually we got to be friends. I even took her to the movies a couple of times." Then he nodded to Kenny. "We sell a lot of your books there, Mr. Thibodeau."

"I wouldn't admit that to anybody, Tommy."

Tommy smiled, but now his body tensed. Hands into fists, his eyes jittery. He gulped twice. He looked around at the melee that was calming down. He was going to tell me something. Then the tension and the anxiety drained from him and he said, "Well, I better get going. I—I'm not real popular with Mr. Mainwaring now. You know, I've kinda lived there for the last year and a half. It was real peaceful there. But I don't think he wants me around anymore. I wanna see if I can patch things up. I hate to be—you know, banned from there for good or anything."

The sadness looked wrong hanging on the beefy teenager. He should be flattening players on the field or pouring himself a sloppy beer at a kegger or making it with a comely cheerleader in the backseat of a car. All that energy, all that popularity, all that raw strength—but now he was stooped again, bereft as an orphan in those Dust Bowl photographs of the Depression '30s. It wasn't difficult to imagine that he'd cried about this—or even that he might cry about it now, as soon as he was out of my sight.

"Did you want to tell me something, Tommy? I kind of got that sense a minute ago."

"Nah—I mean—" After a glance at Kenny and then at me, he said: "I just wanted to apologize."

He turned and left, quickly becoming part of the crowd.

"I wonder what he wanted to tell you, McCain."

"Yeah, I wonder, too."

15

I was working my ass off eating a bagel and reading the morning paper's version of the events that followed Kenny and me leaving the good Reverend Cartwright's play last night. Apparently things had settled down enough for the program to continue. My favorite line in the story was: "According to most estimates, Pearson's Peak is not considered a mountain."

"Did you like the coffee this morning, Mr. C?"

"Great as usual." Jamie was sensitive about her coffee.

"I tried a new brand. I thought you might notice."

I put the paper down. "I was going to mention it the minute I stopped reading. Whatever brand it is, keep on buying it. It's terrific."

Her smile pleased me. I enjoyed seeing Jamie happy. Lately her blue eyes had lost their luster and her slight shoulders slumped. Between motherhood and her surfer-boy lazy bastard husband, she deserved to smile every once in a while.

Which was when our door opened as if a pair of battering rams had been thrust against it. Jamie jumped in her seat, her hands covering her mouth, a sharp noise caught in her throat.

He stood in the doorway with his finger pointed at me as if it was a weapon. "You son of a bitch." Then he glared at Jamie. "Get her out of here. And I mean now."

Jamie was already crying. I hurried around the desk. When my hands went to her shoulders I felt how rigid her entire body was. "Why don't you go somewhere for half an hour or so?"

"But where will I go, Mr. C?"

"The café down the street would be a good place. Get a donut and some coffee. It won't be as good as our coffee, of course."

She didn't laugh, just plucked a Kleenex from the box on her desk and blew her nose—a hardy blow indeed. I helped her up from her chair, grabbed her purse, and slid it under her arm.

All the time our guest stood there trying to restrain himself from attacking me.

"Will you be all right, Mr. C?"

"I'll be fine, Jamie. Now you go on and have a coffee break."

"But it's not even nine yet—"

"Get her the hell out of here right now, McCain."

I walked her quickly to the door. Four steps across from the threshold she started to turn around to say something. I closed the door.

"You son of a bitch."

"You said that already, Paul."

After I was seated again, I said, "You could always sit down."

But Paul Mainwaring was seething. "I should tear your head off, McCain. But I've got stockholders and they wouldn't be happy about the bad publicity."

"Some people wouldn't consider it bad. They'd think you were a hero."

"That's just the kind of glib bullshit I'd expect from you." He was calming down enough to consider using the chair. He eyed it with great suspicion, as if it was about to attack him. "You've been asking a lot of questions that don't need to be asked. Dragging my family's name through the mud. I wanted you to find out who killed my daughter. But for some goddamn reason you started investigating my whole family." He was so angry he was spluttering.

"Sit down and tell me what you're so upset about."

In his blue golf shirt and chinos, he looked like any other millionaire playing hooky from the office. Except for the throbbing veins in his neck and temple. "I want you to stop right now. Period. And if you don't, I'm going to use every cent I have to make sure you won't have any business in this state again. I'm going to file a nuisance suit against you and leak all kinds of things about you to the press. There's a guy in Chicago who is famous for handling cases like this. He's destroyed a number of people. He doesn't care if he wins or loses the case as long as the other guy has to go on relief."

"Sounds like a nice fella. I'd like to meet him sometime."

His rage was back. He pounded my desk with enough power to cleave it in two. Or maybe three. "I'm sorry I ever had anything to do with you. I must have been out of my mind." Then he caught himself. "Twenty thousand dollars."

"Twenty thousand dollars. Nice round sum."

"It's yours if you give me a letter saying that you will never again work on the case of my daughter's murder and will never try to contact anybody even marginally involved."

"Correct me if I'm wrong, but you yourself just said you hired me to find out who killed Vanessa."

"You're not stupid, McCain. But you don't seem to understand that we know who the killer was. He took his own life. There is no more case. And there is certainly no reason to be investigating Eve. She's very upset right now and I don't blame her. Whatever she does with her life is her business. Do you understand that?"

Giving me the impression that he knew all about Eve's lovers. "Yes."

"Yes, you'll sign that document?"

"Yes, I understand why you're pissed and why she's pissed. But I was just trying to do my job."

"So you won't sign the document?"

"No, I won't."

He came up out of his chair with blood in his cheeks and spittle on his lips. "Then you're going to be very sorry. And if you ever approach my wife—or anybody in my house for that matter—I'll have you arrested."

There was no point in arguing. He needed to keep battering me with threats. He was exorcising the demons of a dead daughter, a faithless wife, and now a minor private detective who could besmirch his reputation. Hating me made sense. He'd suffered more than anybody should have with the death of his daughter. I was only adding to his grief.

He leaned over my desk and jabbed a finger at me. "I thought you were a man of honor, McCain. But you had me fooled. You're just another grubby little opportunist."

Again there was no reason to defend myself. If I was an opportunist, I was a badly paid one. And even if I did manage to uncover the real murderer, nobody would be particularly interested past the usual twenty-four-hour time limit before another more interesting crime story came along. The trial would revive interest several months down the line, but meanwhile I'd still be buying my boxer shorts at Sears and trying to find the station with the cheapest gas prices.

"You just remember what I said." But gone was the anger. In its place was only exhaustion. It was as if he, not me, had been the victim of his rancor. He even swayed a bit, like somebody who just might faint on you. His face was streaming with sweat and his shirt splotchy and dark in places.

As I watched him leave, he seemed to be a much older man than the one who'd come here maybe fifteen minutes ago. I heard his footsteps in the hall, slow, even shuffling, and then the exterior door opened and closed. It was several minutes before I heard his Jag fire up.

Jamie returned with a cardboard cup of coffee from the deli. She looked around as if Mainwaring might be hiding someplace, ready to pounce on her.

"He's gone."

"I was ready to call the police, Mr. C."

"I'm fine. He's upset about his daughter dying and it's affected his judgment, that's all. There can't be anything worse than losing your child."

"Oh, God, don't even say that. I look at little Laurie and I want to cry sometimes, thinking of all the terrible things that could happen to her. Sometimes I just want to lock us in a room and never leave so I can keep an eye on her all the time. But I have to go out. And Turk would help but he's, you know, busy with all his stuff."

Yes, too much to ask Surfer Boy to help with his child. I knew I'd soon be having one of those dreams where I separated Turk's head from his shoulders. I knew that broadsword would come in handy someday. Sam McCain, Barbarian.

I used line two to make several calls about pending cases, one in response to a bail bondsman who seemed to blame me for the disappearance of our mutual client.

"Sure, you don't have to worry, McCain. You get your fat fee one way or the other."

"Right. I inherited this stupid bastard from his brother, who told me that while he did have a .38 in his pocket when the cops stopped him inside the supermarket, he wasn't planning to rob it. The only reason I took it is because the county attorney got way ahead of himself here. Even though this dipshit had a gun on him, it doesn't necessarily mean that he was going to rob the place. There's no evidence of that. I decided to help him out because I thought the law was overstepping. I got the county attorney to drop the robbery charge but he didn't have a license for the gun. And he had three priors."

A businessman's deep sigh. "I should've gone into the funeral business like my old man."

"I don't blame you. Getting to handle corpses all day is something I couldn't pass up, either."

A laugh rumbled from the phone. The guy was on the Pall Mall diet. "If you see this bastard, run him over for me, will you?"

"Will do."

As I was hanging up, line one rang and Jamie answered in her clear sweet voice and said, "One moment, please. I'll see if he's available." She put the line on hold and said, "It's Mrs. Eve Mainwaring."

Was she calling to tell me the same thing her husband just had—that I was to stay out of her life? I lifted the receiver and said, "Hello."

"I know my husband was at your office. I followed him."

"Any special reason you're following him?"

"Because he's not himself since Van died and I'm worried about him, what he might do. I was afraid—well, for some reason people don't seem to think he can be violent, he's so easygoing. But I've seen his violent side a few times during our marriage and he can be frightening. And I'm afraid I led him into something— Would it be possible to talk to you? Not at your office. Do you know where the Cotillion is?"

"Sure."

"How about eleven thirty? And don't worry, I'll pay your hourly fee."

"I don't care about the fee, Mrs. Mainwaring."

"We were introduced as Sam and Eve, let's keep it that way. I'll see you at eleven thirty."

As I hung up, I said to Jamie, "I'm going to eat lunch at the Cotillion."

"Petty cash, I'll bet."

One of her many responsibilities was keeping track of the petty cash, never letting it get under fifty dollars. At first I'd been worried she might tell Surfer Boy about it. He'd find a way to con her out of some money. But one day, looking quite happy about herself as she dished out some money for me, she said, "It's a good thing I never told Turk about this. He'd be after me all the time if I did."

The Cotillion was located on a small hill above the river. Before I reached it, I turned right onto a narrow road that hadn't been asphalted in years. I kept thinking about Tommy Delaney and the way he'd waved to me last night, as if he wanted to tell me something. I still wondered what it was.

This time when I pulled up at his white clapboard house that the casual eye might mistake for abandoned—if houses took on the emotional tenor of their residents, this one reminded me of a wound—there was no screaming, no sound at all except for a crop-dusting plane flying low and poisoning the air and the earth. In the backyard I saw Tommy shooting baskets at a hoop attached to a one-car garage. He brought a football player's zeal to making layups. He made three of them by the time I reached him. He was dribbling his way back to start again when he saw me approach. He pawed a right hand across his yellow high school T-shirt. His red hair was in his face, giving him the blunt, sweaty look of a big hearty animal. Only his blue eyes denied the impression; he seemed to be afraid.

"Morning, Tommy."

"You're not supposed to be here, Mr. McCain."

"Oh? Why not?"

As he glanced toward the house I heard the back door slam, and in seconds a scrawny woman several inches shorter than me stalked into view, her hands stuffed into the pockets of her faded housedress. She was leathery and intense and I imagined she could hold her own with that sparring partner she'd married. If she'd had a gun I would have been dead. "You get your butt off my property and leave my son alone." To Tommy: "You go on and get in the house."

He didn't bother to show embarrassment. Mrs. Hitler had spoken and her word was so final it was like arguing with wind or sunlight. He turned into a lost puppy, all sunken shoulders and hanging head,

125

tucked the basketball under one arm, and shuffled toward the house as if he was going to be executed.

"If you're not off my property in sixty seconds I'm calling the law on you."

I could see her as one of those hardscrabble prairie women of frontier Iowa standing with a shotgun defending her roost and her children while her man was away. Read a history of the frontier and you quickly learn that women worked harder than men. "A woman's work is never done" had it right. Consequently, they were not to be trifled with. As was the case with this scrappy, wild-eyed woman.

"I take it you got a call from Paul Mainwaring."

"And so what if I did?" She stepped closer, squinting with a pirate's eye at the intruder. "You're no friend of my son's and Mr. Mainwaring *is*. He helped my whole family since my husband got injured down to the mill. And he's going to see to it that Tommy gets into college. Now you get your butt in that car of yours and get out of here."

Tommy Delaney was watching us from behind the soiled white curtains in the kitchen. He wanted to tell me something. I had no doubt of it.

"All I'm trying to do is find out who really killed Mainwaring's daughter. For some reason he doesn't want me to."

"He said you'd be talking crazy if you showed up out here. And he sure was right. I guess you don't read the papers, huh? That Cameron boy killed her because he was jealous she was seeing other boys. I'm just glad my Tommy got over her. He used to moon around here like a sick calf. I wouldn't say this to Mr. Mainwaring, but it seems to me that Vanessa brought a lot of this on herself. You can't flaunt around the way she did, have all these boys coming after you and treating them the way she did."

"She didn't deserve to die."

In the blue-sky morning, birds bursting from the green, green trees, a sun-scorched cow standing on a distant hill, the little prairie woman was quiet for the moment considering—or reconsidering—what she'd said. "I shouldn't have put it that way. Whatever she did, she didn't deserve to die for it." But pity was not anything to be indulged in. It weakened you. "But she shouldn't have lived the way she did. She made life hell for a lot of people."

I kept thinking about Tommy "mooning around like a sick calf." I needed to talk to him. He'd been part of the Mainwaring family. He might know something that I needed to know.

The phone rang inside. She didn't take her eyes from me. "That'll be somebody calling for me. But I'm gonna stand here till you get in that car and drive off. Now move. You don't have no business here, and if you come back—or you try to talk to Tommy—I'm gonna call Mr. Mainwaring the way he told me to. And then you're gonna be in trouble. He won't fool around with you. He's got the money and the power to put you out of business. And those're his words. Now go."

Tommy came to the screen door in back and stuck his head out. "Phone for you, Mom." He wouldn't look at me.

She didn't have the same problem. She started toward me, stopped and scowled at me a final time. "Now you git."

I scowled right back but I got.

16

The name Cotillion implies debutante coming-out parties and the type of fancy balls where Civil War colonels made plans to deflower the local virgins later on in the gin-crazed night. This particular Cotillion was one of those modern glass-and-stone boxes that were colder than any of the drinks they served. Its reputation for excellent cuisine came, or so I had surmised, from the fact that you paid a lot of money for very little food. This is my small-town side, I know, and when I go out to eat I don't want to gorge myself but I do want something more substantial than two inches of, say, steak covered with oily sauce and topped with some kind of vegetation that looks like a fungus. Not that it tastes bad; it doesn't. The food is tasty, no doubt about it. But even a mouse would ask for his money back when he saw the size of the entrée.

But it is one of the local status symbols to be seen dining here, and the dearth of a substantial meal is often explained this way: "This is how they serve food in New York."

"You mean so tiny?"

"Right. Out here we're raised on meat and potatoes and apple pie. We're used to stuffing ourselves. But this is how people eat in the big cities."

I've heard this conversation, in various formations, for the five years the Cotillion has been open. If somebody dining here ever said, "You know, for what you get, this food is overpriced," the roof would collapse.

While I waited for Eve Mainwaring, I chomped on some bread-sticks I'd swiped from the deserted table behind me. One of the waiters caught me. Instead of anger he flashed me the worst look of all, pity.

She arrived a few minutes after twelve. When people are late the least they can do is rush in out of breath and start their apologizing even before they reach the table. Goddesses are excepted from this rule. In fact, I'm pretty sure there's a constitutional amendment about that.

I'd managed to get a table along the wall that gave us moderate privacy. But I wasn't sure why I'd bothered. She did as much glad-handing as a politician ten points behind on the day before the election. She was chignon-ready with a golden linen dress and two-inch heels that gave her the air of importance she wanted. Given the heat, the other women here wore simpler outfits, comfort being at least as important as style. By the time she reached our table the public smile had become grotesque, as if it had been pasted on like a Groucho Marx mustache.

As with all good goddesses, apologizing was out of the question. She stood by her chair, apparently waiting for me to leap up and be a gentleman, but after she got over that foolishness, she yanked out the chair and seated herself, the smile still in place. "Do you have a match?"

"You want me to give you a hot foot?"

"Are you supposed to be funny?"

"My five-year-old nephew thinks I'm hilarious."

"I don't doubt that. Now be a gentleman and give me a light."

I pitched the matches across the table.

"You are really a disgusting little man."

"Do you want to hear what I think about *you*?"

She lit her cigarette the way a *Vogue* model would—with that perfect angle of head—and then sailed my matches back to me. "I really don't give a damn what you think about me. I know you've been snooping and that's what I want to talk to you about. Or wanted to, past tense. I didn't realize till now that you're one of them."

"Martians?"

"Locals."

"The great unwashed. And you're right, I am one of them."

"Then this will be a complete waste of my time and yours. I came here ready to confide in you but now I'd never give you the time of day."

"You were late."

She sat back and stared at me. Then she began laughing. It was a very merry laugh and I liked it despite myself. The sound conveyed pleasure and irony. "God, is that why you're being such a jerk? Because I was late?"

"You owe me an apology." As soon as the words came out I realized how pathetic they were. An eight-year-old sulking because his feelings had been hurt.

She laughed again, damn her. "Well, then, we'll just have to do something about your little feelings being hurt, won't we? I happened to have had a flat and didn't feel up to changing a tire—which I've done many times, I assure you. I didn't want to ruin this dress which I like, so I had to walk up to a house and ask the woman—one of the 'great unwashed,' as you said—if I might use her phone. She said yes. She was very sweet. I called the service station where we take our cars. The woman let me wait inside and even gave me coffee and a very tasty cookie. Chocolate chip, homemade, if you're interested. I would've called here and left a message for you but I thought the station would send a truck sooner than they did—both their trucks were busy at the same time. But here you were suffering for thirty-four minutes all alone and unloved, cramming breadsticks into your mouth. Flecks of which, by the way, are all over your tie and jacket."

Fortunately, the waiter appeared and I didn't have to respond to her. Her smile was always smug but now it was downright scornful. Before I could get a word out, she said, "I'll have a glass of Chardonnay and this little fellow here will have a Coke. I'm sorry to see he's been sitting here all this time without ordering anything. They tried to teach him manners at the home but sometimes it's a slow process. We'll need more time to decide what we'll want to eat. And do you happen to have a bib he could use?"

The young waiter's face shifted from confusion to amusement and back to confusion. He wanted to smile about all her imperiousness but was that proper when the guy sitting across from her was from some kind of "home"? This could mean anything from cooties to frontal lobotomy.

After he was gone, she said, "I'm pretty sure that Paul will be joining us. He followed me here."

"Why would he do that?"

"He doesn't want me to talk to you."

"I hope he's calmed down some since he was in my office. He was ready for a net and the bughouse."

And then he was there and in the Cotillion. He was a celebrity. By now the restaurant was filling up with credit-card businessmen who recognized the most resplendent of the peacocks among them. Paul Mainwaring. Where his wife had made a ballet out of finding her table, Mainwaring moved relentlessly, flicking nods and waves to people, but never smiles. We both sat silently watching him invade us which he did with dispatch and economy.

"I don't want to make a scene here, McCain. Otherwise I'd pound your face in right now."

"And very nice to see you, too, Mainwaring. And thanks for sparing me the trouble of kicking you in the balls while you were pounding my face in."

The goddess, displeased, rolled her eyes. "Will you two shut up for God's sake? This is ridiculous. And by the way, Paul, I don't appreciate you following me around."

He pulled a padded brown leather chair closer to his wife and sat down. Then his hand went up like a spear and the waiter rushed for us as if summoned by not one but two popes.

"The usual scotch and water, Mr. Mainwaring?" A slight tremor in the young voice.

"Of course."

To Eve, the waiter said, "All we have is a lobster bib, Mrs. Mainwaring. Would that be all right for this—" He eyed me as if I was road kill. "This little fella?"

"Oh, a lobster bib would be perfect."

He started to bow from the waist then caught himself. "I'll bring it back with Mr. Mainwaring's drink."

"Thank you so much."

Mainwaring's eyes had narrowed; his mouth was a bitter slash. The moment the waiter was out of earshot, he snapped, "You're still doing that stupid 'bib' gag? Isn't it about time you give it up, Eve?" He had shifted his wrath from me to his wife.

"Oh, that's right, forgive me. I apologize for trying to have some fun. That's against the rules, isn't it?"

"In case you've forgotten, my daughter is dead. I know you two didn't get along and most of that was her fault but couldn't you at least try to fake some regret?"

The first thing I tried to figure out was how sincere her tears were. They were silver and lovely against her perfect cheekbones, and even the single sob was just as startling as a cynic might say it was meant to be. But there was always the possibility that Mainwaring's words had had their desired effect and had actually surprised and hurt her.

Mainwaring sighed, glanced at me, shook his head, and leaned over to slide his arm around his wife's shoulders. Her head was down now. She was quiet. "Forgive me, Eve. I—I'm just confused and I'm taking it out on you. With Van gone—I don't need to deal with a scandal on top of this."

He put a big hand under her chin and raised her head. The tears were gone from her cheeks but stood in her eyes. She used her starched napkin to dab her nose and then eyes. "And right in front of McCain."

"You were the one who wanted to meet him. I asked you not to." But his voice was sympathetic this time. He kissed her on the cheek.

She placed her hand over his. "But he already knows some of it." She inclined her head toward me as she spoke. "Maybe if we explained things to him—"

He was a man long accustomed to getting his way. Since things weren't going so well now he took his arm from her shoulders and sat there glowering. "Why don't we just get a microphone and tell everybody in the restaurant?"

"I was trying to be helpful, Paul. He's going to find out anyway."

"You think I'm going to sit here while you're telling him?"

Irritation was in her voice and eyes now. "You don't have to be here while I do it if you don't want to. Maybe I can persuade him to see things from our side."

"He's a private investigator who works for Judge Whitney. He's not exactly a good prospect for keeping a secret."

She looked directly at me and said, "Paul and I have an open marriage."

PART THREE

17

So there we had it. Open marriage was something I read about in *Playboy* and the kind of paperbacks Kenny writes. Sometimes you see brief stories about it on TV news but it's always reported as if the newsman is handling feces. Even the swankiest of people—despite the protestations that they love their spouse devoutly and are positive that sleeping around has no effect on the children—come off as selfish and decadent. What's wrong with these people? Haven't they ever heard of plain old all-American adultery?

The sexual revolution, which we heard about as often as we heard the Pentagon lies about the war, had come to Black River Falls, Iowa.

"Well there, you've said it, Eve. Happy now?"

"Oh, sure, Paul. I'm delirious. Can't you tell?"

"Did your girls know about this?"

"What's that got to do with anything?" Mainwaring was ready for an argument.

"You said Vanessa changed after Eve came. I wonder if she ever found out about your arrangement."

"Not that I know of."

"We were very discreet."

"Look at his face," Mainwaring said. "He just can't wait to tell everybody he knows."

"You're right, Paul. I'm thinking of calling Walter Cronkite."

"I'm so damned sick of you. I wish I'd never hired you."

"Believe it or not, Paul, I'm not going to tell anybody. If your arrangement doesn't have any bearing on Vanessa's murder it doesn't matter. But I have to remind you that being discreet in a town this size is difficult. Your friends at the Sleepy Time got guilty and called you, but if they told me, how many other people did they tell?"

"I'll talk to them and they'll be damned sorry. Damned sorry. They needed money a few years ago and were overextended at the bank. I loaned them several thousand dollars at three percent. I can call that in any time I choose."

Again, Eve put her hand over his. "They're friends of ours, Paul. Keep that in mind."

"Some friends."

"I just want to ask one more time—"

Eve spoke before Mainwaring could. "The girls didn't know anything about it. We were very careful. They disliked me simply because I was trying to replace their mother. That happens all the time with widowers."

Not that it could have had anything to do with Eve's personality or the way she treated Marsha or her need to be number one babe in residence.

"Are we about done here?" Mainwaring had taken to drumming his fingers on the table. As chairman of the board he believed that when he was through talking the meeting was over. Who wanted to hear the prattle of lesser beings?

"We haven't eaten yet, Paul."

"Are you really hungry, Eve?"

She bowed her head slightly as if in prayer. I'd just demoted her from a fine actress to a ham. A very clumsy move. "No, I guess you're right. Van's dead and that's all that matters."

Suddenly, soap opera actors looked pretty good to me.

"I told you what I'd pay you to write that letter, McCain. Twenty thousand. Now I want you to add a line about our marital arrangement. That you'll stay silent about that, too."

"I won't write it."

"Then you're a fool."

"No, I'm not. You'll just have to take my word for it. I won't tell anybody as long as it doesn't have any bearing on your daughter's death."

"Which means that you're going to keep on asking questions and putting your nose into things that aren't any of your business."

"That isn't my way of looking at it but yes, I still don't think the Cameron boy killed your daughter. And I don't think he committed suicide, either."

"I was hoping we were going to be friends, Sam. You're making that impossible." I wasn't sure what the word "friends" meant to her, but I was probably flattering myself if I thought there was a hint of lust in her definition.

"Let's get out of here." Mainwaring had taken her arm and popped her out of her seat so that they were both glaring down at me accusingly. "If I see you anywhere around my property, McCain, I'm going to have you arrested."

"You're a very big disappointment to me, Sam," Eve said.

As soon as they started to leave, the waiter returned. "Aren't they going to eat?"

"No, but I am." I gave him my order. "Is there a pay phone nearby?"

"Just off the lobby."

"Thanks."

When Marsha answered, she said, "The Mainwaring residence."

"Marsha, it's Sam."

"You sound as if something's wrong."

"You didn't get this call, Marsha. I just had lunch with Paul and Eve—well, we planned to have lunch, let's say—and they both made it clear that they don't want anything to do with me. So please don't tell them I called."

"All right. I won't."

"I appreciate it, Marsha. Is Nicole there?"

"She's up in her room. She's got a small TV up there and rarely comes down. This morning I brought her breakfast up to her."

"Does she have a phone in her room?"

"The girls each had their own line. I can't imagine what Mr. Mainwaring had to pay the phone company every month."

"Would you mind going up there and asking her if I could talk to her?"

"That's no problem, Sam. But you'll have to call her back."

"That's fine. I just don't want to be on the phone with her when Paul and Eve get back. They wouldn't be very happy to know she's talking to me."

"I'll hurry."

"Thanks again, Marsha."

"I imagine she'll talk to you. She told me she likes you. I'll be right back."

The wait was only a few minutes. "Here's her private number. She said she'd be happy to talk to you."

"Marsha, I'm sending you a Cadillac."

I could feel her smile through the phone. "I'd settle for a new Plymouth. My old one is wearing out. It's ten years old and needs a lot of help. It's sort of like me."

"You sure didn't look like it when I was out there."

"You sure can sling it, Sam. Good luck with Nicole."

While I dialed I thought about Paul and Eve Mainwaring. They had a secret worth keeping. Paul worked in a military environment, and while generals likely had frequent orgies with various animals, the Pentagon made sure that these were considered as top secret as nuclear warhead locations. People with military secrets were blackmailed all the time. Mainwaring had opened himself up to that and to being tainted with the stigma of perversion if his behavior was made public.

When Nicole came on the phone, she said, "My father is going to be mad I talked to you."

"I know that. And he may well be on his way home right now. I had lunch with him just a few minutes ago."

"I don't give a shit what he thinks, Mr. McCain. I just said that to warn you."

"Is there a place we could meet around four o'clock?"

"I ride my bike up to Whittier Point a lot. There's a pavilion up there. I like to sit in the corner of it and read."

"That'd be great. Four o'clock, all right?"

"I'll be there."

I spent the next hour and a half in the office working on a probate case. Somewhere at midpoint the phone rang and Jamie said, "It's Commander Potter, Mr. C."

Potter said, "You won't like me after this call."

"What makes you think I like you now?"

"Very funny, asshole. Paul Mainwaring just left here and he's convinced the chief that you're to be arrested if you keep bothering people about his daughter's death."

"What would he arrest me for?"

"He'll figure out something. He'll haul you in and then you'll bail out and then he'll haul you in again when you start bothering people again. And so on. Why don't you save yourself and me a lot of trouble and just give it up?"

"Maybe because I'm onto something."

"Uh-huh. If you were on to something you'd have called me about it already."

"You make a lot of assumptions."

"Just give it up, Sam, because I'm the one who'll have to bring you in and that won't be fun for either of us."

"I can't do that, Mike."

"Well, then I can't keep from arresting you." And with that he hung up.

I went back to work on the probate case, more distracted than ever. Mainwaring was moving in on me now. As Potter had hinted, this was nothing more than harassment. But Mainwaring knew many powerful people in this state, including the governor himself. If Mainwaring wanted to call in some favors, he could. For relief I kept glancing at my wristwatch. I had an hour and a half before I drove out to Whittier Point. At least the scenery would change.

The probate case I was working on was ridiculous but modestly profitable so I'd taken it. When their old man died, leaving two thousand dollars and a shotgun to his daughter, his son came to me and said he wanted to contest it. This seemed curious to me because the son was a prominent psychiatrist in Iowa City. He'd grown up here with his old man and his sister. It was the latter he was after. According to him, the old man had always favored her. She got all the new clothes, all the money to go east for college and, more than anything, all the love and support because she reminded his father of his late wife. He was close to tears while he was telling me, biting his lip and twisting his hands. I felt like the shrink listening to a patient. I wouldn't be recommending his services to anybody I knew.

When I heard Jamie say, "Oh, hi, may I help you?" I raised my head and stared straight into the eyes of Sarah Powers. She and another girl stood in the doorway of my office, both looking nervous.

"Hi, Sarah."

"Hi." Sarah wore a blue work shirt and jeans. She held a cigarette aloft with great delicacy, the ash at least half an inch long.

"Let me help you with that," Jamie said. Seconds later she slid an ashtray under the cigarette. Sarah flicked the ash and thanked her.

"This is Glenna, Sam. I wondered if you'd talk to us. Glenna knows something about what happened the night Vanessa died." Glenna was a thin, tall girl with blond hair in a ponytail and quick, suspicious brown eyes. Her T-shirt read STOP THE WAR NOW!

"Sure. Come on in."

Jamie dragged an extra chair in front of my desk so both girls could sit. Glenna's fringed buckskin shirt had to be damned hot on a day like this. When she sat down she leaned back and dragged a package of Winstons from the front pocket of her jeans. The pack was pinched by now so that when she got a cigarette out she had to straighten it up.

"Glenna just came to the commune a couple of weeks ago. She's a real good cook. She made a pumpkin pie last week that knocked everybody out. Plus she's got her college degree. But she dropped out of society just like the rest of us because it's all such bullshit."

That remark caused Jamie to show some interest in the conversation. She stopped her typing to listen. The remark caused me to force a somber look on lips that wanted to smile. The casual way so many of them said "we dropped out of society" had always struck me as funny. They shopped at grocery stores, they had cars that needed repairs, some of them had to pay light and gas and phone bills, and they weren't averse to going to doctors or free clinics. They'd dropped out of the parts of society they didn't like but they were very much still citizens.

"And she saw Vanessa go into that barn."

I straightened up. This required full attention. "What time was this, Glenna?"

"She says it was right after supper. She was going to the barn to see if this kitten had come back. She found this little black-and-white one—"

"Sarah, why don't you let Glenna talk?"

Sarah blushed bright as an autumn apple. "I'm sorry. But she's shy. She asked me to do the talking."

"I'm sorry. I need to hear it from her."

She took a deep breath. "She, uh, thinks you're like, you know, one of the pigs."

"Why, that's not true, Sarah. Mr. C isn't a pig. You shouldn't say things like that," Jamie interjected.

"If that's true, she should tell me I'm a pig herself."

"You're a pig," Glenna said.

"All right, now that we've got that established, how about telling me what you saw that night."

"I'm only doing this because I know Neil never murdered anybody. That's something only pigs do. Neil was transcendental and so am I."

"Good enough. So what about Vanessa that night?"

"I saw her behind the barn. She was arguing with Richard."

"You could hear them arguing?"

"No, but it was obvious. She sort of shoved him once and started to walk away but he grabbed her by the arm."

"They didn't see you?"

"I was over by that old silo. They couldn't see me in the shadows. Plus it was starting to get real dark."

"How long did you watch them?"

"Probably ten, eleven minutes, something like that. Until she ran inside the barn and he went in after her. That time I did hear them—at least, I heard him shout her name. I didn't want to get involved because Richard thinks we spy on him anyway. He can get real paranoid."

"Why didn't you come forward before?"

This time she took a deep breath. When she exhaled the sound was ragged, anxious. "I got in a little trouble in Iowa City. I'm on probation. I don't want to get hassled by the pigs again."

"What happened in Iowa City?"

"They can't take a joke is what happened in Iowa City."

"That doesn't exactly tell me anything."

"Go ahead, Glenna. Tell him."

"It doesn't matter, Sarah."

"Sure it matters. So please tell me."

"I puked into this bucket and then threw the bucket at a cop. I got vomit all over him. All we were doing was trying to take over this dean's office. This dean was a real pig."

The hell of it was she seemed to be serious. I wasn't sure how to deal with someone who didn't understand that throwing a bucket of puke at somebody just might be considered an aggressive and unlawful act. "Can't imagine why the cop'd be pissed off about that."

"I'm glad you never try to be sarcastic. I told you he'd be a pig, Sarah."

As I'd said so many times, most of the hippies I'd met over the past few years I'd liked. I agreed with them about the war, about the materialism of our society, about the alienation so many of us felt. Just as there were a few hippie haters in town, there were also a few hippie lunatics and right now I was sitting across from one of them.

"All I care about right now is that you'd be willing to testify to what you just said. Under oath."

"I don't think so."

"Hey, Glenna, you promised me you would."

"I said I 'might.' But I don't like this jerk. At all."

"Forget about him. He doesn't matter—no offense, Sam. What matters is that you're willing to admit the truth to the cops. And save my brother's reputation."

"Well, if I do it, that's the *only* reason I'll do it."

"That's all I care about," I said. "Sarah, I'll leave it up to you to hold her to this. The first thing I need to do is talk to Richard. This doesn't mean he killed her."

"See what I mean, Sarah? That's why I didn't want to come here. He's already making excuses for Richard. They're big buddies."

"She hates Richard, Sam. She thinks she should be running the commune."

Somehow that's not a surprise, I thought. But I didn't say it, of course, not with Rasputin sitting directly in front of me.

"He thinks he's so cool," Glenna said.

"She used to live with Richard."

"He doesn't believe any of the things he says about the revolution," Glenna said, managing to light a cigarette while saying this. "He has two credit cards."

"Maybe he needs them," Sarah suggested quietly.

"You think Lenin had credit cards?"

"I need to get out of here. I have some appointments. One of them will be to go see Richard. In the meantime, Sarah, I'd appreciate it if you'd make sure that Glenna is willing to tell her story to the authorities if need be."

"That's cool. Now he's not talking to me. He's only talking to you."

But Sarah was already dragging herself and Glenna to their feet and didn't respond. I think that she was as tired of Stalin's daughter as Jamie and I were.

"I'll talk to you soon, Sam."

"Thanks, Sarah. And thank you, too, Glenna. I appreciate you helping us like this." *You crazy bitch.* But of course that was a thought meant only for me, myself, and I. Like Sarah, I had to abide Glenna's nastiness in order to ensure her testimony.

At the door, Sarah turned back and gave me a frown, a shrug and a nod toward Glenna, who was preceding her into the hall. I wished she had drawn an invisible circle around her head, the way people do to indicate that somebody is nuts. But then Glenna just might have been packing a flame thrower and melted Sarah down on the spot.

After we heard the outside door open and close, Jamie said, "That woman scares me. And she shouldn't have talked to you the way she did."

"Well, she'll be helpful to us if Richard was involved as she claims."

"Turk thinks hippies should be put in prison. He says they don't contribute anything to society. And he says boys with long hair are nothing but girls anyway and make him sick."

Let's see. Turk the wife-abuser, Turk the willfully unemployed, Turk who lives off his wife's work, Turk the leader of Iowa's only surfer band, thinks hippies should be sent to prison. It seemed that the ones who hassled hippies the most were the bikers, the local thugs, and the hillbillies from the Hills—you know, the cream of local society. No surprise that Turk was among them.

"I just say live and let live, like most people around here do."

As I was passing her desk, I bent over and kissed the top of her head.

"Gee, thanks, Mr. C." The blush just made her all the cuter.

I was about out the door. In fact, I was one step over the office threshold when the phone rang. When I was four steps over the threshold and making my way to the outside door, Jamie said, "It's Mr. Federman. Do you want to talk to him?"

"Hey," he said. "I call at a bad time?" The people at the Wilhoyt agency were always polite.

"No. It's fine. Just real busy."

"Well I found out two things that might interest you. Eve, original name Sharon Carmichael, has been named in two different divorce cases by very unhappy wives. She has also been married to two wealthy older gentlemen. She got a small sum from one when he kicked her out for cheating on him and nothing from the other one because he threatened to send around the photos his private investigator snapped of her. Her name was variously Sharon Downes and Sylvia Tralins. I got this from two newspapermen. Just thought you'd like to know. Should I keep digging?"

"Definitely. I just wonder if Mainwaring knew about any of this."

He laughed. "The way you described how hooked he is—you think it would've made any difference?"

18

The commune was busy. Four or five people worked the sprawling garden, two two-man units were fixing drainpipes and a front door and two women were washing a van vivid with peace symbols in various colors. Grace Slick was urging people to violence (from her safe posh digs on the West Coast, of course) and a dog was yipping his disagreement. I wanted to shake his paw.

As I walked to the front porch of the nearest house a few people looked me over and apparently decided I wasn't worth even sneering at. A Negro kid named Jim Ryan came out the front door carrying a toolbox. He was tall and fleshy but not fat. A few of the more ardent racists in town had hassled him many times. One time he decided to hassle them back. It turned into another case where Cliffie wanted to charge him but the county attorney's office said no, he'd just been defending himself. The good people of the town, who far outnumber the bad, wrote many letters to the newspaper talking about the "riffraff" that had picked on Ryan and given Black River Falls a name it didn't deserve.

Ryan had been one of those rare perfect clients—bright, quiet, amenable to following my instructions. Today he wore his "Power to the People" T-shirt and jeans. He smiled when he saw me. "Lot of people around here don't seem to like you much."

"It's the same in town, Jim."

He set the toolbox down. "I used to build homes in the summers. I collected a lot of stuff. You lookin' for Sarah?" He was talking loud, over Grace Slick.

"Donovan."

His dark eyes changed expression. "He's been in his room since early last night. He doesn't want anybody to bother him. I knocked once last night and he called me a bunch of names. Pissed me off. He's a nasty son of a bitch, way he runs this place. I'll be moving on pretty soon. Can't hack it here any more with him around."

"Any idea why he's holed up?"

"You're askin' the wrong guy, Mr. McCain. I never could figure him out except he's a jerk. I admit we need a leader here just to keep things running right. But we don't need an egomaniac."

A woman came out wearing a craftsman's denim apron. She must have been in charge of the music because it died just as I heard a "See you in the barn, Jim." She glanced at me. Her lips flattened into displeasure. She hurried on.

"Another admirer."

"They think you didn't defend us very well from all the bad publicity. Not all of them think that, not me and the majority. But some of them. They're lookin' for somebody to blame because they think maybe they'll all have to move because of some of the people in town. I kept tryin' to tell them that there wasn't anything you could do. But you know how stoners are."

"I guess I don't."

He grinned. "Sometimes they make me ashamed I enjoy drugs as much as I do."

The interior of the house had been cleaned up and painted. The furnishings in the front room came from the Salvation Army or someplace similar. The old stuff has faces—the weary couch, the tortured chair, the wounded ottoman. It was no different upstairs where air mattresses and sleeping bags ran three or four to a room. The smells ran to pot and smoke and wine and sex. A kitten so small she would have fit in the palm of my hand accompanied me as I tried to find Richard Donovan. The walls of the hallway were colorful and baleful with posters of Che, Bobby Rush, Nixon, and Southern cops.

My search ended at the only room with a closed door. I tried the doorknob and found that it was also locked. I knocked: "Richard, it's McCain. Open up."

So our little game began. I'd knock and he'd stay silent. I had my usual rational reaction to impotence; I kept rattling the doorknob. It would magically open; I just knew it.

Finally, he said, "I don't feel like talking. Just go away."

"If I don't talk to you, I'll talk to Mike Potter."

"Is that supposed to be a threat?"

"I've got a witness who saw you arguing with Vanessa right before she was killed."

The silence again.

"You hear me?"

"Yeah, I heard you all right and I bet it was that bitch Glenna who told you, too."

"Doesn't matter who it was. Now open up."

After a long minute he was in the doorway, shirtless, barefoot and sullen. He was doing a James Dean, his hands shoved deep into his pockets. From what I could see, his room was clean and orderly, almost military in the precise way he'd laid it out. "So we argued a little. That's all it was."

"What did you argue about?"

"That's none of your business."

"I'm told she shoved you and started to walk away but you grabbed her by the arm and then followed her into the barn shouting her name."

"You know the kind of lawyers my old man has access to? He'd take some bitch like Glenna apart on the stand."

"You're not convincing me you didn't kill Vanessa."

He leaned against the doorframe as if he might fall down if he didn't have support. His eyes went through three quick and remarkable expressions—anger, hurt, fear. "I shouldn't ever have hooked up with Glenna. She's psycho, and I mean completely. Jealous of any girl who even looked at me."

"That why you broke it off with her?"

"I can't believe she still hates me. That was almost six months ago."

He took a minute to jerk a pack of Marlboros from his back pocket. He knew how to stall. He set a world record finding a book of matches in the other back pocket, then getting the smoke lit. "I had a little thing with somebody."

"Vanessa."

His body tensed at the mention of her name. "She and Neil were having problems."

"So you stepped in."

"She wanted it." The absolute lord and master of the commune was whimpering now. "I saw her in town one night and we ended up going to a movie in Iowa City. A French flick. She was a pretty cool girl for a hole like Black River Falls. Then we just started seeing each other—you know, on the sly." His gaze fell away from me. He got real interested in how his cigarette was burning. "I didn't want Neil to find out. I didn't want him to think I was moving in on his chick."

I forced the laugh back down my throat. "Yeah, you wouldn't want him to think anything like that."

This time his eyes tried to put burning holes in my face. "We were friends."

"You're a noble son of a bitch, no doubt about it."

He moved back and started to slam the door but I was too quick. In a past life I must have sold encyclopedias. I had my foot planted in front of said door and it wasn't going anywhere. "What happened when he found out?"

"Who said he found out?"

"Don't waste my time. Of course he found out. It's hard to sneak around in this commune or in town for that matter. Somebody must have spotted you."

He touched his forehead with the fingers that held his cigarette as if somebody had just driven a railroad spike into it. "Glenna followed me one night. She saw us and told Neil. He—" I wasn't sure if the shrug was meant to impress me or himself. "He was crazy. He threatened to kill me. Then I didn't give a damn about him anymore. And neither did Van. She was afraid of him, in fact."

"Leading up to the night she was killed."

"What?"

"You still haven't told me what you were arguing about with her."

"*You* know every goddamn thing. How about you telling *me*?"

"That she didn't want to see you anymore and that there wasn't any point in bothering her the way you had been."

I wasn't sure if it was an illusion or whether his face had paled.

"That seemed to be the pattern. Whenever the guy got too close to her she got scared and walked away. And that's what happened to you, too, wasn't it?"

The scowl didn't work because he looked tired now. "You think whatever you want. But you better have some proof. Like I said, McCain, my old man has some very prominent lawyers. They'd eat you alive."

"I wouldn't go anywhere if I was you."

The scowl hadn't worked but he had more success with the smirk. "Sure thing, little man."

I withdrew my foot. The door slammed shut. I wondered how long it would take him to call his old man. The prodigal son returns home. In bad need of a big-time mouthpiece.

Whittier Point was in favor when it was used by the kids of a grade school a block away. Then the grade school was consolidated with a

larger school and Whittier Point was left to lie fallow. The city kept
the grass mown on the area around the large pavilion but all the playground equipment was gone. Without supervision the city would be
asking for a lawsuit; hell, even with supervision there'd been lawsuits.
Hot weekends families still trekked up here, but on workdays it was
often empty except for school-age lovers lost in their own obsession
with each other.

Until nearly four thirty my only companions were quicksilver birds
lighting on the empty picnic tables and two stray dogs who kept their
noses to the cement floor as if uranium might be found under it.

For the first time I considered Richard Donovan a real suspect.
Neil Cameron had been his rival for Vanessa. He'd been seen arguing
with her not long before her murder. And he'd gone rich boy on me
when I'd asked him if he'd killed her. Telling somebody you're going
to get world-class lawyers to save you doesn't inspire confidence in
your innocence.

And naturally I wondered why Nicole wasn't here yet. Maybe she'd
changed her mind. Maybe she'd decided that she'd angered her father
enough already by talking to me.

I got up and started walking around the area outside the pavilion. The
birds had that day's-end sound, and a cordial, solemn weariness seemed
to settle on the trees and grass and the small lake just over the west side of
the hill. There were moments when I wanted to be a kid again, hurrying
home to my collection of paperbacks and comic books, the only realm in
which I was really myself. My dad would still be alive and he and my mom
would be laughing about something adult just as I entered the kitchen and
asked when supper would be ready. I could even put up with my bratty
sister, whom I loved despite all my protests to the contrary.

Then I saw her.

The winding paved road ended in a steep grade if you wanted
to veer off and reach the pavilion. But she rode her ten-speed with
energy and skill. As she drew near she waved; the gesture was girly and
sweet. But then the front tire swerved and she was quickly dumped
on the grass.

I ran over to her. She'd been thrown facedown but she was quick to roll over on her back with her arms flung wide. She was gasping for breath. Her eyes fluttered as if she might faint. I knelt down next to her and felt her racing pulse. Her breath still came in bursts and a whimper played in her mouth.

"I guess I should've taken the car." That she'd managed the sentence with such clarity reassured me she was all right. Still, it was strange that a girl of her age, in apparent good health, would be worn out to the point where she'd lost control of her bicycle.

I helped her to her feet and looked for any cuts or scrapes. She fell against me for a moment. I slid my arm through hers and walked her into the pavilion and sat her down. "I'm throwing your bike in my trunk and giving you a ride home. No arguments."

"They'll see us together."

"I'll let you off a ways before your estate."

"God, this is so embarrassing."

"It's still ninety degrees. Could happen to anybody."

"Our house isn't even a mile away." She touched her face. Body heat had emphasized the acne on her cheeks. Her white blouse was soaked in spots.

"I've got a cold Pepsi in the car that I've had about half of. How does that sound?"

"That sounds great."

She drank it in sips, which was smart. The drink relaxed her, or seemed to. She leaned back and took one of those deep breaths that usually mean you're feeling better—even philosophical—about some problem. "I guess it was kinda stupid on a hot day like this." Then: "My dad *really* doesn't like you."

"That I know. But why did he kick Tommy Delaney out?"

She wiped her brow with the back of her tiny, corded hand. "Poor Tommy. I always liked him but I don't think anybody else did. Except Marsha. She told me one day how bad it was at home for him. His folks always argued and sometimes it got violent. I guess his whole life was like that. She said that was why he liked being at our place so much. It was peaceful and it made him feel special, you know, with my dad being so wealthy and all. The funny thing is, it was my dad who started inviting him over. He'd show him off to his friends. He always gave a speech, too, about how Tommy was going to put the Hawkeyes in the Rose Bowl. But Eve hated him. She thought he was a moron. And that was the word she used. She worked on Dad until he started to dislike Tommy, too. I guess when Van was killed he decided it was a good time to get rid of Tommy."

"Tommy's not handling it too well."

She fanned herself with her tiny hand. "That's what I figured. He really isn't some big dumb jock. He's real sensitive, you know? I think he was in love with Van for a little while but he was smart. He gave up right away. I mean, it was hopeless. Then he fell in love with Sarah. Van wouldn't even listen to him when he was telling her that Neil was sorry for being so mad all the time and how much he loved her. Tommy felt sorry for Neil, that's why he stepped in. But I told him up front it wouldn't work."

"Why not?" But my question came automatically. I was thinking about Tommy being in love with Sarah.

"She wanted to humiliate Dad every way she could. And that meant being with a lot of boys. But I doubt she slept with more than one or two of them. She told me she hated sex because it reminded her of Dad."

"And this was all because your dad married Eve?"

"Well—" She perched herself on the edge of the bench. She pursed her lips, looked away for long seconds then said: "There was something else, too. But now it doesn't matter. Van's dead."

"Did this thing that doesn't matter anymore affect you the same way it affected Van?"

She inhaled deeply through her nose. "I really don't want to talk about it, all right?"

"It might help me."

"My dad said it's all over. That you're only out to embarrass him."

"At one time your dad and I were close to being friends."

"That isn't the way he remembers it."

There was only one way in. "Does Eve go out much at night—alone?"

Getting to her feet was an effort. She wobbled on the first two steps. I caught her wrist gently and eased her back.

"Please let me go. I really don't want to talk about this."

"I just asked you if Eve went out alone at night sometimes."

"What do you want me to say? Yes, she did."

"How about your dad? Did he go out at night alone sometimes, too?"

"Of course he did. And still does. He's an important man. He has to." She broke suddenly, hands to face, quick dagger of a sob. "You know about their arrangement, don't you?"

"Was that why Van hated him so much?"

This time she had no trouble standing. Or walking. She walked down the wall and finally seated herself on the low ledge at the end of it. She didn't say anything for a time. She wasn't crying now. She didn't even look upset. When she looked at me all she said was, "I need a cigarette."

I did the movie star thing and lighted smokes for both of us. I carried them down and gave her hers. She had her nice legs stretched out in front of her now. She was considering them. She didn't seem to have much pride in herself. I hoped she at least realized that she had perfect coltish legs.

She smoked eagerly. "How did you find out?"

"Right now that doesn't matter. How did you and Van find out?"

A bright smile. "We followed her. Private investigators. We wanted to get something on her. We thought maybe Dad would divorce her if we could prove to him she was unfaithful. And that was pretty easy. She went out with Bobby Randall several times. And we assumed there were others, too. It's funny how it worked out, though."

I waited until she was ready to talk again.

"Before we got to tell him, Van and I got the flu pretty bad. We were in bed because we were so sick. I was asleep late one night when Van came into my room. She was so sick she could barely talk. She said she'd started down the stairs to get some orange juice and then she heard something she couldn't believe. I was so groggy I wasn't even sure what she was talking about. She said that this party Dad and Eve were having tonight—the men were drawing numbers to see which one of them would sleep with another man's wife. I couldn't understand it at first. But Van wasn't just beautiful, she kept up on things. She said this was what they called wife swapping and she said Dad was having a great time. They were going to pair off, then get together that weekend at Dad's house up on the river. It's three stories and sort of like a hotel. Then Van started crying. I helped her into the bathroom so she could throw up. She was that sick—sick about what Dad was doing. She got into bed with me—I used to do that to her when we were little. She just kept crying and I held her and rocked her and sometimes I'd cry, too."

She turned and flipped her cigarette onto the lawn. "That was a couple of years ago and that's when she started running around. She'd never been like that before."

"Did you or Van ever confront your father about it?"

"Oh, sure. We could tell he was embarrassed. He promised he wouldn't do it anymore. We both wanted to believe him. But then after about a month or so he started going out alone at night the way Eve kept doing. We followed him. He went to the same motel Eve did. The women were wives of his friends. Van used to scream at him and threaten to kill Eve. She always said that Eve shouldn't ever have been allowed to live in the same house our mom did. I agreed with her completely. Completely." Then: "Pretty shitty, huh?"

"Pretty shitty." I don't know why I was surprised that the Mainwarings had lied to me about the girls not knowing.

"He said we'd understand better when we were older. But neither of us believed that. That isn't any way to live. It's like he's in his second childhood or something." Then: "I guess I'll take you up on that ride back home."

"You want to head back now?"

"Yes, maybe I'd better. I'm really wasted for some reason."

I remembered how she'd been in my car the other day, not at her best, either. But there were a variety of physical responses to loss and trauma.

"You feel up to walking now?"

"I'm not a baby." Sharp, angry.

"I was just offering to help."

"I know, it's just—I'm sorry. I shouldn't have snapped at you like that. I hate being bitchy."

"I can't imagine you bitchy."

Her whooping laugh was directed at me. "You're one of those guys Van always told me about—the ones who idealize girls. You don't want to be around me when I get bitchy. I was even worse than Van and that was pretty bad."

"Thanks for the warning. Next time I'll come armed."

A soft summer giggle. "Well, I didn't say I was *that* bad."

With that she shoved off the edge of the wall. "Thanks for everything, Sam. I really appreciate it."

I put my hand on her shoulder. "Let's go get your bike."

19

Three hours later I sat in a chair on Wendy's patio watching the day slowly fade into dusk. Wendy had given me a kiss, a beer, and a promise that even though dinner would be late it would be something I really liked. She would meanwhile go visit her mother for no longer than an hour. Whenever her mom felt that nobody was paying her sufficient attention she had panic attacks designed to get her noticed. Since Wendy's sister lived in Portland, Oregon, it fell to Wendy to be the noticer.

Dusk is always a melancholy time for me and I've never been sure why. Sometimes I feel the loneliness that has always been my curse, a loneliness that nobody can assuage. Tonight for company I had Wendy's hefty cat Victor. He sat in the chair next to mine and swatted at everything that tried to assault his bastion from the air. He had yet to down a single firefly but he certainly kept trying.

I wanted to give myself up to the Cubs game that was just getting started on the radio. Misery loves company and nothing is more miserable than listening to the Cubs blow another season. But this was pregame yak and so I was left to the dying day.

It would have been nice to send my mind on vacation so that I could just sit here and be one with my surroundings but I was restless. I kept thinking about the night of the murder. None of the lovers Van had thrown over would have had a difficult time getting into that barn—there was easy access through the thin line of forest in the back. Anybody who'd followed her to the commune would have been able to swing wide and enter the barn without being seen.

I also thought about the effect Eve had had upon the girls. Imagine if you'd grown up with a sweet, attentive, understanding mother who died and was replaced by a stunning but vapid swinger. And even worse, that your father became a swinger, too. Hey, one Frank Sinatra is enough for this planet, man. Had Eve taken her vengeance out on Van?

Victor started purring when the back door opened, which meant his mistress and patroness had come home. She carried her drink on a blue cloth coaster over to Victor's chair and nudged him aside so that she could sit down. He went unwillingly. As soon as she was seated he jumped on her lap.

"Feeling any better?"

"Not really. So much up in the air."

"I ran into Mike Potter at the supermarket. I bought us some red snapper we can put on the grill tonight."

"He tell you I'm crazy?"

"More or less. And he's worried that you could get in serious trouble with the state if you keep pushing this."

"I just want to make sure we get the truth."

"I said that to him. He said, 'If Sam wants to waste his time it's up to him.' But he smiled when he said it."

"That was nice of him."

"How about a back rub on the bed?"

"Are you trying to seduce me?"

"Maybe. Or maybe I'm just trying to distract you. You need to take a break."

We fit just about perfectly as lovers. And when we finished, Victor was squatting on the bureau and watching us in the darkness scented with Wendy's perfumes and sachets and creams. We'd had an audience.

"I never did get that back rub."

"Too late, buddy. I'm going to grill us some red snapper. And you're going to set the table."

"This is just like the National Guard I go to once a month. Too many orders."

"Don't say that. They're talking about drafting you guys. I saw it in the paper this morning. You must've seen it."

"I'll start setting the table."

"So you're not going to talk about it?"

"They've been predicting that for two years now. I'll set the table."

I went inside and started grabbing plates, glasses, silverware, and nap-kins. I was careful to limit myself to the second-best of everything. The plates had tiny chips and the shine was off the silverware. I didn't blame her. Her only real asset was this house she owned. She basically lived on the income from the trust her husband had left for her. It had been the largesse of a decent but guilty man. Not his fault that he'd fallen in love with one of the girls his bully-boy father would never have approved of. He'd married Wendy because he was fond of her and because his family approved of her family. The trouble was that Wendy had been in love with him and had come undone when he'd been killed in Nam.

And Nam was on my mind now, as well. Not only because I opposed the savage, meaningless war—Ike's "military-industrial complex" warning coming true in spades—but also because our post commander at the guard had given us notice that we might be called up. I'd lied to Wendy. Nam was in the offing. A number of guard units had already been sent there. At the rate our troops were being killed, the great dark god that was slaughtering the lives of soldiers and innocents alike was ever hungrier. It wanted more flesh and blood, and many of the men in the guard were at the right age for making patriotic sacrifices the chickenshit politicians could prattle about when reelection time came around again.

But talking about it with Wendy was difficult. Her husband had died over there. And that's what worried her, the cheap irony of losing her first husband and then her husband-to-be in the same war. I didn't blame her for the dread she faced in her nightmares but I also couldn't do anything about it. Maybe we'd luck out. Maybe we wouldn't be called up. But as General Westmoreland told more and more lies, and more and more of our troops died, I didn't know how we would be spared.

She came in and opened the refrigerator. She slapped two pieces of red snapper on the counter and started preparing them for cooking. She was fast and efficient and fun to watch. She didn't say anything.

"You not speaking?"

"No, because if I do speak you know what I'll speak *about* and then neither of us'll feel like eating. You know how worried I've been about it. The story in the paper just made it official."

"Maybe it won't happen."

"Just let me prepare this fish and not think about anything else."

A good meal and two glasses of wine later we both felt momentarily invincible and loving. We sat in chairs on the screened-in back porch and held hands like high schoolers. Victor appeared and sat on Wendy's lap. The only music was the night itself: the breeze and the faint passage of cars and the even more distant sounds of airplanes approaching Cedar Rapids for landing. I felt old and logy and I didn't mind it at all. I even considered the possibility—combine alcohol and fatigue and you can come up with the damnedest thoughts—that maybe, just maybe, things were exactly as they appeared. Neil Cameron killed Vanessa Mainwaring because he felt betrayed by her. And then he killed himself. Judge Whitney wouldn't be happy with this because Cliffie would have won one. And even one would be too much for Judge Whitney. The Sykes clan represented all things evil to her.

"How about helping me clean up and then we go to bed?"

"Fine. As long as you can help me drag myself up from this chair."

"You were supposed to help *me*, Sam." She laughed. "God, we sound like we're eighty years old."

"Speak for yourself. I don't feel a day over seventy-five."

"I love this so much. It's so comfortable with you."

"Is that another word for boring?"

"What an ego. You just want a compliment."

"I love you so much because you're so 'comfortable.' Not exactly inspiring."

She giggled. "And because you're so exciting to be with and such a stud in bed and because all my girlfriends are jealous that I've been able to keep a heartbreaker like you interested in little ol' me."

"Much better."

"*Now* will you help me clean up?"

I concentrated on the grill and she worked on the dishes. When I came inside she was just loading the dishwasher. "See, that didn't take long." She tossed me a towel. "How about I wash and you dry? I've still got these pots and pans to take care of."

The kinds of relationships I'd had with women in the past had been all sex and tension. Lots of breakups and makeups. There hadn't been time in all the groping and battling to get domestic in any way. Wendy and I were already married in an informal sort of way. But sometimes I got scared it would all end for some terrible reason.

She jabbed me in the ribs. "You haven't seemed to notice but there aren't any more pots or pans to dry. You've been standing there with that last one for a couple of minutes now. You must be thinking of something really fascinating."

"I'm just hoping this doesn't come to an end any time soon."

"You keep asking me to marry you and you say something like that?" She smiled and kissed me. "Look, Sam, I worry about the same thing. And that's why I just want to wait a little while. We're crazy about each other. I want to spend my life with you. But I just want to be careful about it." She took pan and towel from me and set them on the counter. "Maybe we'd better discuss this in the bedroom."

By the time we finished making love, neither of us had enough energy left for discussing anything. She fell asleep against my out-stretched arm. The aroma of her clean hair was innocently erotic.

The call came at 3:26.

The phone was located on the nightstand on Wendy's side of the bed—as was only right; it was *her* bed—and before I was completely aware of what was going on, she had the phone to her ear and was talking. She'd told me once that all the while her husband was in Nam, where he eventually died on his second tour, she had nightmares about the phone ringing in the middle of the night and a cold military voice telling her that her husband was dead. She told me that she woke up several nights to find the phone in her hand, a dial tone loud in her ear. She'd incorporated the nightmare into reality.

"It's Mike," she said, lifting up the Princess-style phone and planting it on my stomach. I took the receiver and listened. I asked him to repeat what he'd said, so he went through it once more. He said he was at the crime scene and that if I wanted to join him it would be all right. He said that Cliffie wouldn't be there; he'd called the chief but the chief felt that Potter could handle it. I could sense Potter's smile when he quoted Cliffie: "I think you've learned a lot from me since you've been here and I've let you handle a number of other things already. You just keep me posted—the morning's soon enough." This was the first time I'd heard Potter draw down on Cliffie. But it was late and the scene he was at had to be a true bummer.

"What's going on?" Wendy whispered. Since I was still talking to Potter, I held up my hand to wave her off.

"I'm on my way, Mike."

Wendy had slipped into the bathroom. I heard her pee and then start brushing her teeth. If the National Dental Society or whatever it was called wanted to give a trophy (a big shining jewel carved into a tooth) to the person who brushed her teeth the most times a day, Wendy would be their choice. Seven, eight times a day and that doesn't count flossing.

I got a light switched on and dressed. I used one of her hairbrushes to batten down my own dark mess. I was lighting a cigarette when she came out wearing a ragged old robe she liked. She managed to look tousled, sweet, and very sexy.

She came over and took my cigarette from me. She inhaled deeply, exhaled in a blast. She held up a finger. "One more." After she finally gave me my smoke back, she said, "Mike sounded shaky. What's going on?"

"Tommy Delaney," I said, "hanged himself earlier tonight."

20

Cue the rain.

Halfway to the Delaney residence a hot, dirty summer rain shower started pelting my car. I had the radio turned up to KOMA in Oklahoma, still my favorite station. In the middle of the night this way the signal was stronger than during the day. A bitter anti-war song seemed right for this moment. I kept lighting one cigarette from another. I resented all the snug people in their dark snug houses as I passed street after street.

All the natural questions came to me. What had Tommy Delaney wanted to tell me and then backed away from? Was this going to be another murder disguised as a suicide? Had he left a note explaining everything?

The Hills had never looked better, the darkness a mercy to the crumbling houses and sad metal monsters parked curbside, all cracked windshields and rusted parts and political bumper stickers for men who had only contempt for the owners. The closer I got to the Delaney place the more lights I saw in the small houses. The people inside would have heard the sirens and seen the blood splash of emergency lights pitched across the sky. Most would have stayed inside; after all, it was raining now, and who wanted to get wet? But the vampires among them would have shrugged on raincoats and trudged out. Pain, misery, and death awaited them, and this was a tasty brew that would give them a fix of the life force they sought.

The local press was already there. The cops had shunted them to a corner of the action. A beefy part-time deputy stood next to them to make sure they didn't stray. I parked next to the ambulance and walked over to where Mike Potter was giving orders to another part-time deputy. The crowd numbered somewhere around thirty, not a sell-out crowd but not bad for a rainy four a.m. show that wasn't in 3-D or Cinemascope.

The air smelled of wet earth, exhaust fumes from all the vehicles, and a cancer ward's worth of cigarette smoke, my own contribution included. Two squad cars sat together shining their headlights on the front of the garage. The door was down so all I could see was the blank white wood with rust snaking down from the roof. Above the door was the basketball hoop where I'd seen Tommy Delaney shooting baskets that day.

As I approached Potter I heard a scream from inside the house. The piercing agony of it stopped me as I think it stopped everybody who heard it. I'd been surveying the scene the way an investigator would. The scream forced me to survey it now as a simple human being. No doubt one or both of the parents had found their son hanging from a crossbeam in the garage. A madness would set in. They would blame themselves, they would blame him and they would blame existence itself, a ramble scramble of rage and grief and even more rage. I'd worked with enough social workers to know how suicides like this played out.

Potter said, "I'd stay away from his folks if I was you."

"They mentioned me?"

Rain pattered on his police cap. "According to her, her son was a nice, easygoing kid until you started pestering him about the Mainwaring girl."

"That's bullshit."

He had a flashlight the size of a kid's baseball bat in his hand. "C'mon, I'll take you into the garage."

On the way in, I said, "Did you hear me? What she said is bullshit. I came out here twice. Twice. That's hardly 'pestering' him or whatever she said. In fact, I'm pretty sure he wanted to talk to me about something."

"Then why didn't he?" The cop guarding the side door stood aside as we approached.

"How do I know why he didn't?"

"But you're sure he did? He sent you some kind of mind message?"

The sarcasm ended the minute we stepped inside. The hard-packed dirt floor, the rain and cool air streaming through the glassless window frame in back, the smells of gasoline, oil, and dirt, now joined with vomit and feces. Somebody had run the only car outside so that the police could bring in all the necessary equipment to nail down every aspect of the suicide.

The way Tommy's mouth was twisted, it was almost as if he'd been smiling when death had taken him, a grotesque smile that seemed fitting for his end. He wasn't twitching, anyway, twitching the way he'd been with his folks screaming behind him in what was likely their ongoing marital war. I remembered the tic in his left eye and the forlorn, beaten tone of his voice. Their voices would have been with him as he'd looked for shelter and solace somewhere else. The Mainwaring home would have provided that.

All he wore was his jeans; no shirt, no shoes. Puke streamed down his chest and his right foot had been splashed with his runny feces.

"He left a note."

"Let's talk outside."

Potter raised his eyes, studied Tommy for a time then looked at me. "Yeah, outside."

The rain was backing off to a drizzle and the action was slowing down to the point that some of the ghouls, soaked, were wandering home. The hardiest of them would stay to see the corpse inserted into the ambulance.

I felt somebody watching me and when I looked to my left I saw Mrs. Delaney hiding behind a kitchen curtain. Even from here her hatred was clear.

"I got on a ladder and climbed up and looked at the ligature marks, Sam. No doubt about this one as far as I'm concerned. He definitely killed himself. The M.E.'ll examine him and make absolutely sure it's suicide."

"I didn't have any doubt about this one."

"Why not?"

"For one thing, the little time I spent with him he struck me as a pretty sad kid."

"Hell, he was a football hero."

"Not when you heard his parents shrieking at each other. I stood on the front lawn and heard them. Tommy was coming apart. It was like shell shock. And that came from years of listening to them trying to destroy each other. The other thing was he wanted to tell me something—at least that was the impression I had. But he could never quite do it."

"Any idea what it was?"

"No. But he knew a lot about the Mainwarings."

He lighted a cigarette now that the rain wouldn't soak it. The smoke smelled good in the chilling air. "That note he left, he apologized to his parents for taking his life and asked them to pray for him. And then he said that he never had any luck with women and that he just couldn't go on."

"And that's all?"

Before he could answer, the back door screeched open and barked shut. I saw her coming at me. Nuclear warhead. No confusion about who she wanted and what she planned to do.

Potter saw it, too, and stepped in front of me. "Mrs. Delaney, I asked you to please stay inside."

She pointed a witch finger at me and screamed: "He killed my Tommy! He wouldn't leave him alone! Tommy was scared of him! Tommy'd be alive if it wasn't for him!"

"Please, Mrs. Delaney—please go back inside. This isn't good for you or your husband."

But it was great for the living dead, the remainder of the group already pushing their way toward the garage. Drama was almost as good as blood.

She flung herself at Potter, trying to get her hands on me. "He should be the one who's dead! He should be the one who's dead! He killed my Tommy!"

Paralysis. I couldn't move, speak. I was afraid of what I might have done to contribute to Tommy's suicide—maybe he felt pressure to tell me something but was afraid to and my contacting him scared him— just as I was afraid of her. All that anger, all that sorrow. I wanted to say something to comfort her but anything from me would sound blasphemous now.

"Just let me tell him to his face!" She dove at Potter but a stocky, balding man in a Hawkeye T-shirt came up from behind her and put big workingman hands carefully on her shoulders and began the inch-by-inch process of extracting her from Potter's body.

He just kept saying, "C'mon now, honey; c'mon now, honey," the way you might to a small child you were trying to soothe. Soft words, loving words. Hard to imagine this was the same man I'd heard battling this woman when I came here the first time to talk to Tommy. This time he was saying the right thing in the right way.

When he finally drew her to him, she folded herself into his arms and wept. He put one of those big hands on the back of her head and began stroking her gently. This made her weep even more.

This time the paralysis wasn't just mine. Potter stood in place, too, just watching her collapse into her husband's keeping. Not even the ghouls said anything, or moved. I thought of a documentary I'd seen about a tiger cub born dead and the mother trekking the corpse nearly a hundred miles across scorching, dusty Africa. Not wanting to ever give it up. Mr. Delaney showed that kind of ferocious protectiveness as he slowly guided her back toward the house. He kept muttering his mantra. She clung to him with a desperation that made them indivisible.

Potter said, "Nothing with kids. And Tommy was a kid."

We'd had this conversation a number of times, how he could handle just about anything but death scenes involving kids or young people. He said he'd seen too many such scenes in Kansas City. He never elaborated on any of them.

Then he got brisk and officious. He wanted to wrap things up. The M.E. could get here and give his benediction and then every-body—except one unlucky uniform—could go home and catch what remained of sleep before the six-thirty alarm clock.

The remaining ghouls began to fade. A light went on in a back room. Shadows against a cotton blind. A piercing sob, then silence. The light went out.

"I hope this is the end of it," Potter said. Irritation was clear in his eyes and voice. "No more murders or suicides. My wife keeps reminding me that we moved out here to take it easy. Now my migraines are back, I'm downing a bottle of Pepto a day, and I'm constipated."

"Pepto constipates you."

"I know, but it's either that or having heartburn that damn near knocks me out."

I stared with great longing at my car. It would take me away from here. I would be back in bed with Wendy. In the morning the sun-light would be golden and pure and maybe we'd make love in it and then have breakfast on the back porch and Wendy would be sweet and fetching and for a time I wouldn't have to think about every-thing that had happened in the past few days or whether Wendy was going to marry me sometime soon. Or if my National Guard unit would be called up for the war that was a farce and a cruel joke on the American people.

"You be sure and keep me posted if you hear anything," Potter said.

"I will."

As I walked to my car I saw Mr. Delaney in one of the kitchen windows watching me. I almost waved. Instinct. But in this instance waving would be more than slightly inappropriate. I got one quick good look at his face. He seemed to hate me as much as his wife did. Maybe more but he couldn't express what he was feeling the way she did. He just stared.

In my car I snapped the radio on. Then right back off. Wrong to listen to the radio somehow. Instead I smoked and drove fast. Very fast. I didn't go back to Wendy's, I just drove. It was one of those robotic driftings I went through occasionally. Wasn't aware of where I was driving or what I was seeing. Just driving, the act itself lulling me into a state where nothing mattered but the present moment—my fortress against any kind of serious thought.

The first time I became aware of where my car was taking me was down on D Avenue where the Burger Heaven and the second-run theater used to be. There'd been a used-paperback store there for a while, too. And a tavern where they kept their pinball machines in front so teenagers could play them and not get carded or thrown out. It was all gone now. A supermarket and a new Western Auto took up most of the block. No comfort in those.

Wendy was asleep on the couch in her pajamas when I came in. The TV was on and snowy. Victor dozed on the armchair. I went into the kitchen and got myself a beer and sat down in the breakfast nook.

She came in soon enough. "I tried to wait up for you." Sliding into the booth across from me.

"You should've stayed in bed."

"You ever think I was worried about you?"

"If you're so worried about me why don't you just say you'll marry me?"

"Boy, you're in one hell of a mood."

"If you say so."

"All right, I'll marry you. You set the date."

"Are you serious?"

"Yes. I've been thinking about it. We love each other and even though I'm scared about it I don't want to ruin everything by putting it off. I just realized that if you ever walked out the door I would be miserable for the rest of my life."

"Well, probably not for the rest of your life."

"Goddammit, you're in a bad mood. I tell you I love you and that I want to marry you and you just keep on bitching about things."

"Well, I'm happy about it. Of course."

She was out of the booth before I could say anything more.

"Go to hell, Sam. I don't want you in my bed tonight. You take the couch."

Then she was gone. It hadn't done me any good to take Tommy's suicide out on her. I gave it twenty minutes and then went into the dark bedroom and told her how much I loved her. She laughed and said, "I was wondering when you'd show up. Now get into bed."

21

I was in court the next morning. A divorce case. By the time of the trial I'd come to pretty much hate both of them. Selfish people who'd forgotten that they had two very lonely and frightened little girls to take care of. He'd told me, quite earnestly, that as soon as the papers were signed it was "Nookie City for this guy." There are men who could have pulled it off and made you smile along with it. He wasn't one of them. He was, I suppose, good-looking in a big-guy sort of way but he was as vain as a starlet, always combing his hair and watching his biceps pop in his short-sleeved shirts.

One time when he was in my office, I went to the john and came back to find him sucking in his gut and putting the moves on Jamie. She was wily enough to say, "My dad wears the same aftershave you do." A thirty-eight-year-old self-described stud ("Hey, chicks dig me and Elaine could never understand that, the bitch.") being compared to a God-only-knows-how-old Granddad-type? He got back to business, which meant running down his ex some more and winking at me every time he mentioned "chicks." Number one, I hate people who wink and number two, his winks looked like tics.

The judge, a man who had no time for Judge Whitney or me, called me to the bench and leaned over and whispered: "Am I right in thinking that these two are among the biggest assholes who've ever appeared before me?"

I nodded. "Thank you."

He settled mutual custody on them and ordered both of them to take parenting classes. They sputtered and spluttered and called "outrage," in the middle of which the judge brought the hammer down, stood up, and left.

"Parenting classes? Who does that asshole think he is?"

"Maybe you'll meet some chicks there." I grabbed my briefcase and got out of the courtroom fast so I wouldn't have to talk to him anymore.

The sun was so hot at ten thirty I had a science fiction image of people staggering down the sidewalk and falling into the street, their hands waving desperately in the air like drowning victims. I smoked a cigarette and took my time getting back to the office. I passed at least six people who told me how hot it was. I wouldn't have known that otherwise.

My office is located in the rear of a building that has been many things up front. The current tenant who took the front section and thus eighty-five percent of the entire place was an auto parts store.

I walked alongside the building and when I turned I saw Jamie sitting on the steps leading to our office. She had tears in her eyes. She smoked a cigarette and sniffled. When she saw me she just sat there. No signal of recognition.

"What're you doing out here, Jamie?" I said.

"He told me to sit out here."

"Who's he?"

"Mr. Mainwaring."

"What the hell's going on?"

Her blue eyes shone with tears. "I just did what he told me, Mr. C. He scares me."

"So he's inside now?"

"Uh-huh."

I took her hand. "It'll be all right. Why don't you take an early lunch and do a little shopping?"

"Will you be all right?"

"Never better."

"I really don't like him, Mr. C."

"I don't either. But now he's my problem, not yours. Now go have some good food at the deli and put it on the office account."

"Are you sure that's all right?"

"Well, I've talked to the owner of this here law office and he said it was fine with him."

She was picking tears off her cheek with a little girl finger. And now she smiled. "I always tell people you're the funniest man I've ever known, Mr. C."

I didn't have to walk all the way into my office. He half dived out of it to grab me before I reached the threshold. He used his size to shove me hard against the hall closet. "Where is she? Where did you send my daughter?"

He'd become a grotesque. The blue eyes were crazed and the words were cries. Drool trickled from the left side of his mouth. He was slick with sweat and it wasn't from the heat. And then his hands reached for my throat. I tried to push off the closet door but he was too quick. I could feel the fingers on the sides of my neck. I had just enough room to knee him in the groin.

He didn't fall down, he just went into a crouch. He turned away from me so I couldn't see his misery. Even in this situation he was a man of great pride.

I went into my office and sat down at my desk. I pretended to be fascinated by all the pink phone slips waiting for me. He was resourceful. In less than a minute he started groaning out insults. "I'm

going to see that you're in prison for a long time, you little bastard."
And: "If she dies, you'll be an accessory to murder."

That one got my attention and bothered me. "What the hell are
you talking about?"

"At least own up to what you did, you slimy son of a bitch." The
voice was stronger now and he was out of his crouch. As he came
through the door he winced with every step. But his rage was as good
as several shots of bourbon. "I don't know how you could ever be so
goddamned irresponsible. I knew you were dirt, McCain, but she's a
seventeen-year-old girl."

He sank into Jamie's chair. His ferocity was wearing him down.
He stretched a hand to her desk as if for support. The next sound was
a wail. "He'll kill her."

"Paul, damn it. Look at me. Tell me what you're talking about."

"You know damn well what I'm talking about. She's going to have
an abortion because you told her to."

"Paul, that's crazy. I didn't even know she was pregnant."

"Oh, sure. I suppose you didn't see her yesterday afternoon,
either."

"Yeah, I did see her. And what we talked about most of the time
was how she and Van learned that you were doing the same thing Eve
was and that you were in a wife-swapping group. And how much she
and Van hated it."

"Don't put the goddamn blame on me. This is your fault. She's
looking up some butcher who'll abort her. She doesn't know about
sleazy things like that. That's your territory. You and your great friend
Neil Cameron. He's the one who seduced her."

I had my elbow on the desk. Now I rested my head on my hand
and took a deep breath. There are moments when the brain can't—or
refuses to—comprehend and process all the information it is presented.
Pregnant. Abortion. Neil Cameron. My voice sounded mournful.
"What makes you think she's looking for an abortion?"

"She told Marsha she was having one and was driving over to see
some guy. This was about twenty minutes ago."

"Oh, God."

"No shit, huh? Finally sinking in, McCain? Maybe having second thoughts about what you told her?"

I slammed my fist so hard against the desk top that I numbed my hand. "I didn't know she was pregnant and I sure as hell didn't tell her to get an abortion. Do you understand that?"

For the first time clarity came into his eyes. The lunacy waned. "Then who told her about this abortionist?"

"I have no idea. And even if I get around with lowlifes sometimes, I don't know anything about an abortionist in Black River Falls. There was one but he's doing time in Fort Dodge."

Wailing now. "Then where is she?"

"Shut up for a minute."

I grabbed the receiver and started dialing. Kenny answered on the third ring. At this time of day he'd be working on his portable type-writer slamming through "Cannibal Warriors of the Third Reich!" or something similar.

"Yeah?" He did not like being interrupted.

"I've got a big problem here, Kenny, and I'm really in a hurry. Is there anybody you know of who's peddling abortions these days? I know it's been quiet since Thompson got sent up to Fort Dodge for killing that girl."

"Supposedly there's some guy in Milburn. His name is Windom or something like that. I don't know that for a fact. But I heard it from one of the kids who always comes out here to get his copies of my stuff autographed."

Even Kenny was a star of sorts. "That's all you know?"

"Yeah, I'm sorry, that's the best I can do."

"Thanks, Kenny. That's a start anyway."

Mainwaring was on his feet. "What did he say?"

"Milburn. Some guy named Windom. But he says the only way he heard it is that some kid who wants his books autographed told him."

"People want that trash autographed?"

This coming from Mr. Open Marriage and Mr. Wife Swap. But now wasn't the time to respond.

We took his Jaguar. Milburn was fifteen miles away. We both smoked. Any time we pulled up behind a car or truck Mainwaring leaned on the horn as if he thought they'd be so afraid that their vehicles would just take flight and clear a path for us.

"If he laid a hand on her, I'll kill him."

"First of all, we don't even know that he's the guy. So it would make sense to stay a little cool until we find out."

"You don't give a damn, she's not your daughter."

"No, but believe it or not, I like her and I don't want some butcher cutting her up."

All I got was a snarl.

Despite the heat, autumn could be seen in the hills, the tips of trees burning into golds and browns and reds and that scent of fall on a few vagrant breezes. For all the stupendous colossal magnificence of the Jag, the damn air conditioning wouldn't work so we had the windows down.

Milburn runs to maybe fifteen thousand and is known mainly for the Pioneer Days celebration it throws on Labor Day, complete with costumed people and a lot of artifacts from the middle of the last century. It gets a lot of state press, and some big national advertisers sponsor a good share of the expenses.

As we entered the town limits I had the feeling that the place was a big old dog lying on its side in the boiling heat. The shopping district, which ran four blocks, showed a lot of empty parking spaces and only a few people on the sidewalks. A tractor was ahead of us at a stoplight so Mainwaring went into one of his rants about how hillbillies should be shot–stabbed–set on fire for getting in the way of the movers and shakers who by divine right were running this planet. Since (A) farmers aren't hillbillies and (B) I'm pretty sure that there had to be some hillbillies in my bloodline dating back to the early 1800s, I started thinking about shooting–stabbing–setting *him* on fire.

Finally I saw a Sinclair station and said, "Pull in."

He swept the beast onto the drive and I was out the door, him shouting, "What the hell are you doing?"

I like gas stations—the smells of oil and gas and the clang and clank of the guys working on cars in the garage. I like good old gas station conversations, standing around and saying nothing much with a Pepsi and some peanuts and a cigarette with some other guys who are also saying nothing much. This time all I wanted was a phone book which, in the case of Milburn, was about as thick as a comic book.

The middle-aged guy in the green uniform who came out of the garage wiping his hands on a rag looked like the man to ask. "Can you tell me how I'd find Sullivan Road?"

"Sure. Easy to get to from here. You go down two blocks to the Woman's Shop—big store right on the corner—and you turn right and go straight for—let's see—eight blocks. Maybe nine. Anyway, Sullivan Street is off that road there. You'll see a street sign."

"Thanks."

"We don't see many of those around here."

He meant the Jag. "Yeah, but the air-conditioning doesn't work."

He had a great midwestern grin. "You're kidding."

" 'Fraid not. Well, thanks."

"You took long enough," Mainwaring said when I got in the car.

"Shut up and listen."

"I'm not used to people telling me to shut up."

"Tough shit. Now listen."

I gave him directions. They were easy to follow but we went through the honking again. I wanted to find Nicole, too, but without a siren on the Jag, other vehicles just weren't going to shoot up on lawns to get out of our way.

Sullivan Road was where houses went to die. Most of the homes were built in the '20s from what I could see, two-story white clap-boards adjacent to garages not much bigger than closets. Porches leaned and chimneys toppled and shutters hung crooked. On a few of them you could see porch swings that hung from only one chain. The cars were also old, blanched colors and monster rust eating its way across the length of the vehicles.

"This is just the kind of place I expected it'd be," Mainwaring said.

"We're looking for Seventeen twenty-four."

"Some rathole."

"We're on the sixteen hundreds now."

"If he's touched her, I'll kill him."

"You already said that. There's Seventeen-oh-two."

"There's her car!"

The way he grabbed the door handle I thought he was going to leap out of the car before he even slowed down. There was a space across from Nicole's silver Mustang. Mainwaring pulled in. I had to grab his shirt as he tried to vault from the car. "We don't know what we're walking into here. So let me handle this, you understand?"

"Take your hand off me. This is my daughter you're talking about."

"Yeah, well if you're so concerned about your daughter, then we go in there cool and calm." He was so pissed I reasoned that the only way to get his attention was to shock him. "What if he's operating on her? He hears us breaking in and he slips and makes a mistake? You want to be responsible for that?"

His eyes closed tight. An anxious breath. "Oh, God, my poor little Nicole."

"I'll handle things. All right?"

"All right."

"Let's go."

The white picket fence around the scorched grass leaned inward, in some spots so low it was only a few inches from the ground. The gate was missing. The walkway to the door was cracked into jagged points. A variety of animals had used the east side of the lawn for a toilet. Apparently the right side didn't have any toilet paper.

Mainwaring dragged himself now, as if afraid of what lay ahead. He must have still been thinking of the image of the abortionist's tool slipping when he heard our invasion. He muttered to himself but I wasn't sure what he was saying.

In the short distance between the car and the screenless screen door I was already soaked with sweat. We were going to hit ninety-four today according to the dubious wisdom of the weatherman.

There was a bell but I stuck my hand through the frame of the screen door and knocked. The neighborhood was quiet. The loudest sound was the power mower we'd passed about half a block away.

I knocked again. This time a male voice behind the door said something. Then the man who I assumed owned the voice did a foolish thing. He went to the east window and edged the dirty white curtains back and looked out. Straight into my face. I jabbed a finger at the door. The curtain dropped back.

Just to annoy him I knocked again. This time he opened the door. He was a short, heavyset man who had more hair on his body than a papa gorilla. A white T-shirt only emphasized the thick, hirsute chest and arms.

"Help you with something?"

Mainwaring's strength was sufficient to hurl me off the low doorstep and grab on to the hairy man with enough force to drive him back inside so fast I didn't have time to quite understand what was happening. I piled through the doorway right behind him. By now Nicole, who was seated on a badly soiled light blue couch, was pounding on her father's back as he bent over to smash his fist again and again into the hairy man's face. The man was on his knees. His face was already bloody.

I pushed Nicole aside so I could slam my fist into the side of Mainwaring's head. But he had true madness on his side. He was gone into a realm where only murder would satisfy him. Prisons are filled with men like him, men who pay for a single explosive moment with long stretches behind bars.

The hairy man was crying and pleading. Mainwaring didn't stop hitting him until I kicked him so hard in the back of his left knee that he slowed and turned just enough for me to hit him almost square in the face. The hairy man was smart enough to slide away.

Nicole was back on the couch, sobbing now, sounding as crazed as her father, striking her fists against her thighs again and again.

I shoved Mainwaring toward her. "Take care of your daughter."

Dazed, he stumbled toward the couch and sat down next to her. He still didn't know what to do. He just sat there, still trapped in the vestiges of his rage. Then she surprised both of us by throwing herself into his arms and finally he was her father again, and he held her and began crying along with her.

I followed a trail of blood dots on faded linoleum to a small bathroom where the hairy man was splashing water on his face and cursing with a good deal of eloquence.

"That son of a bitch is gonna be payin' me a lot of money by the time I get through with him."

"Are you Windom?"

He whipped around and glared at me. "No, I ain't Windom. Windom moved about four months ago when me'n the missus moved up from Anamosa. She's at work and this is my day off from the railroad." He put a hairy paw to his nose. "This look broke?"

I stepped closer. "Doesn't look like it but I'm not a doc."

He was still trembling. So was I for that matter.

"I'm gettin' me a lawyer."

"I don't blame you. I'll help you find one. I'm Sam McCain." I put my hand out and he shook after hesitating. Blood bubbled on the left side of his mouth. "You need to go to an emergency room and get checked out. What's your name, by the way?"

"Ryan. Nick Ryan."

He grabbed a towel, wincing as he wiped his face. "Bastard is lucky I didn't have my glasses. I can't see much without 'em." Finished drying his face, he said, "She ain't been here but maybe fifteen minutes and I didn't know what the hell she was talking about. She said she was in trouble and didn't I know what she meant. Then she started cryin'. If the wife was here she woulda known what to do but you know how it is when women cry—especially a young one like her—I just got her a bottle of pop and an ashtray. Young kid like that, I felt sorry for her. Then her old man busts in and tries to kill me. What's this Windom s'posed to have done, anyway? This is the second girl come here since we moved in."

"He supposedly performed abortions."

"I'll be damned. I don't go for that, you know. Catholic."

"You go to the E.R. and they can bill Paul Mainwaring."

"Who the hell is Paul Mainwaring?"

He squinted at me when I laughed. "A very important guy. Just ask him."

"Well, I hope he's rich because I'm gonna sue his ass off. We need to fix this place up, that's why we got a deal on it. Place we had in Anamosa was real nice but then the job shifted down here. I make a good living."

"I've got an uncle on the railroad. He makes a lot more than I do."

"Yeah? Whadda you do?"

"I'm a lawyer."

This time the laugh was on me. "You should work for the railroad like your uncle. Honest work."

"Believe me, I've thought about it. Now let's go back to the living room."

I led the way. Mainwaring was helping Nicole to her feet. I said, "You owe this man a sincere apology. And you're going to pick up his E.R. tab. And unless you can make some kind of settlement, he's going to sue your ass off."

"He's an abortionist."

"Now you've slandered him, too."

"I told you, Dad, Mr. Ryan's been very nice to me. He didn't know what I was talking about when I said I needed help."

Mainwaring's eyes roved from hers to mine. "This is true?"

"No, we're making it up because we're all scared you'll go crazy again. Now apologize to him and then give him a ride to the E.R.

and then come to an agreement about how much money you're going to give him." I glanced at Ryan. "I'm his lawyer."

"That's a surprise."

"I'll drive myself home, Dad."

"Can I trust you?"

"How about you? Can I trust *you*?" This was one of those questions carrying a load of history with it—Eve, open marriage, wife swapping, and alienating his two girls.

"Just go straight home."

"You're forgetting something," I said to him. "I don't have a car here. I'll have to ride with Nicole."

She took the keys from her purse, zipped the purse shut, and then looked at me. "Maybe you should drive, Sam. I'm still shaking."

"Just hope that Mr. Ryan doesn't have any serious injuries, Mainwaring."

"Oh, great, now I'm the villain."

"Yeah," I said, "as a matter of fact, you are." If I'd been a sadist I would have used the moment to tell him what I'd learned from the Wilhoyt investigators about his wife. But as much as I disliked him, he had more than his share of grief. I didn't want to add to it.

Nicole, in her peasant skirt and blouse, led me out of the Ryan home. As we walked to her car she said, "Maybe he's learned his lesson. Maybe he'll change."

I didn't want to give her odds on that but I said, "Yeah, maybe."

I drove at about half the speed Mainwaring had a bit earlier. For a time neither of us spoke. "Van and I used to play a game. We used to sit in the back of the car when Mom and Dad would take us someplace and look out the back window at license plates. For weird ones, you know. One time we saw one that read 'I'm cute.' We laughed about that the whole way to Cedar Rapids." Her voice was wistful but pained.

After a time she said, "He wants to send me to my aunt's house till I have the baby. Then we'll adopt it out. That's what he says now, though. I'm trying to imagine having a baby and giving it away."

"You want to go to your aunt's house?"

"Yeah. Even Sarah said I should go away, I mean before she told me about Windom. She said I should go away to school for a year. Try to forget everything."

"She told you about Windom?"

She patted her face as she sometimes did. Maybe she was hoping that her acne had magically disappeared. I used to have moments like that—daydreams—about being taller. "She's my best friend. When I told her that Neil and I snuck around and saw each other for a month, and then I told her I was pregnant, she said I should see this Windom and get an abortion and go away to school. And try to forget everything. I think the whole thing made her mad. She said that Tommy was going to beat Neil up for her but she stopped him and said she'd take care of it." Then, "Poor Tommy. He was kind of a little boy in a lot of ways. But he was so sweet." Her eyes glistened. "And Van and Neil—it's just all so screwed up."

"You don't hold anything against Neil?"

"I want to but I can't." Her gaze was distant now. "I knew he was with me just to make Van jealous. I even told Van about it. But she didn't care. She thought it was funny. She didn't know I was p.g. though. But it was my fault as much as his. I always saw all these really handsome guys around Van. I guess I just sorta wanted one for myself. You know, with my face and all. He was a lot of fun, too. Took me places and made me think about things I never had. He was brilliant. He really was."

"You need to see a doctor right away."

"I know. I've been afraid to go. I'll probably go to Iowa City, where nobody knows me."

"Fine."

"You know, I have a little crush on you. Not a big one. But a nice little one."

"Well, that's funny because I have a little crush on you, too. Not a big one. But a nice little one." Her laugh made us both feel better.

I pulled up next to my car in the small lot behind my office building.

She reached out and took my hand. "I hope I see you again."

"Me, too. And for what it's worth, I think you're wrong about not meeting any more handsome guys. I have the power to see into the future and from what I can see there're a lot of them waiting to take you out."

"I sure hope you're right."

I slid out of the car and started toward my door. Behind me she said, "Thanks for everything, Sam."

By the time I reached the commune a hot rain was storming across the prairie with mean intent. Humans and animals alike rushed to shelter. Lightning walked the land on glowing spider legs and thunder shook the earth. I pulled as close to the houses as I could and then started my own rush to get out of the rain.

With everybody inside temporarily the voices were almost as loud as the music, this time the Beatles' best album, *Rubber Soul.* I had to use a fist on the door to get any attention. A white kid in something like dreadlocks came to the door. I told him who I wanted to see and he gave me a thumbs-up. Maybe in a past life he'd been a WWI ace.

I took one of the two broken-back metal chairs on the porch and had myself a smoke. The laughter from inside was clean and young, and I felt envious of them. Crazy and pretentious as some of them were, at least they were questioning the conventional wisdom of growing up, entering the nine-to-five, and setting aside money for your funeral when you turn forty-five.

I watched the rain drill the flower-power bus and the other wrecked-looking vehicles. A sweet dog face could be seen underneath the bus, all wide-eyed and floppy-eared.

Then she was there. "God, this rain doesn't even cool things off, does it?"

"I wonder how old Cartwright is doing up there waiting to hear from God."

She took the chair next to me. "Sometimes I feel sorry for him, Sam."

"I would if I didn't know he was such a con artist. Hair tonic and diet crap and all that."

In her denim work shirt and jeans she was tomboy comfortable and purposeful. That was my impression, anyway. Except for the eyes. She couldn't hide her anxiety. I guessed she knew why I was here.

"Mainwaring and I followed Nicole this morning. She was under the impression she was going to have an abortion."

The old confrontational Sarah scoffed at me. "You're not exactly being subtle. As far as I'm concerned, I gave her good advice and I don't give a damn if you like it or not. I've seen too many girls her age ruin their lives by getting pregnant."

"So have I. But that's not what this is about."

She leaned away from me. "Oh? So what's 'this' about?"

"I think you know."

She was quick, starting for the door before I got out of my chair. I'd never get her out of the ruckus inside. But then she turned and came back. I had the feeling she was as surprised by her move as I was.

She sat down again. I started to speak but she held up a hand for me to stop.

"I can't get over Tommy killing himself."

"Why do you think he did it?"

"Because of me. Because he was in love with me."

"And you weren't in love with him?"

She dropped her head, was quiet. "I loved him enough not to marry him."

"I don't know what you mean."

She sat back and ground the chair around so she could face me. "He wanted to run away and get married. Not even finish high school. I told him he was crazy but Tommy—Tommy got obsessed easily. Plus he just wanted out of his house. He used to cry like a little kid when his parents had had one of their battles. I hated them for what they'd done to Tommy. But I still wouldn't ruin his life by marrying him right now. I told him he should take one of the scholarships—he had three or four colleges offering him full rides because he was such a good football player. If we got married his life would be ruined. I loved him too much for that."

"So Tommy killed himself because you wouldn't marry him?"

"I don't like your tone there. You trying to say I'm lying?"

"Not at all, Sarah. I believe you. But maybe there was another reason Tommy took his life. In addition to you not marrying him, I mean."

"Well, then I sure don't know what the hell you're talking about."

"I'm talking about him knowing that you killed Neil after you found out that he got Nicole pregnant. You knew Neil had killed Vanessa but you decided to keep his secret. But then when Nicole told you about her pregnancy—" I tried to take her hand. She slapped mine away. "Nicole told me how angry you were when she told you about sleeping with Neil. But I noticed you didn't speak up for Neil quite the same way even before you found out about Nicole. It wasn't anything obvious, but your tone definitely changed. I knew then that you were sure that Neil had killed Vanessa. I can't read your mind but I think it was probably then you realized that your brother was out of control and that he was going to keep right on doing what he'd always done. I cut him a lot of slack for what he saw in Nam, Sarah, but I suspect if you're honest you'll tell me that he was always this way growing up, smashing things and smashing people. That's the way it was, wasn't it?"

"You don't have any right to talk like that. I thought you were my friend."

"I am your friend, Sarah. I care about you. I just think you'll feel better if you tell the truth. There's been too much lying already."

She raised her head and stared at the ceiling of the porch. A whimper became a small sob. "He was my brother. He'd had a hard life. I loved him."

"I know you loved him. But you saw that he needed to be stopped. And when you found out about Nicole, you decided you didn't have any choice. You killed him and tried to make it look like suicide."

She picked up my package of Luckies from the arm of my chair. I handed her my matches. When she got her cigarette burning she handed them back.

"You don't know any of this for sure."

"I do now. And you know it, too."

"He attacked me."

"I don't believe that but it'll make a good defense."

"I don't want you for my lawyer anymore."

"That's a good decision."

"I thought you were my friend," she said again.

"I am. That's why I'll get you the best criminal defense attorney I can."

"I don't have any money."

"It can be worked out." I had no idea how at the moment but there on that porch at that moment it was the right thing to say.

"I didn't plan on doing it."

"All right."

"Don't you believe me?"

"Yes. But you'll have to work this through carefully with your lawyer."

She exploded from her chair as if she'd been blasted out of it. She stalked to the east end of the porch and lowered herself onto the railing. She inhaled hungrily. The tip of the cigarette was an evil little red eye. "You don't know what it was like with Neil. All our lives. He was always in trouble. He was in a fight or he'd stolen something or he'd smashed up something. I used to feel sorry for him because I loved him so much. He always said that people wouldn't accept him for who he was and that's why he was always in trouble. He was just paying them back. For a long time I believed that. But when he got into so much trouble in the service—"

"You mean what you told me about Saigon?"

"No. When they got back stateside he started stealing stuff from the other soldiers. Watches and jewelry they'd bought for their girl-friends and wives. One of them caught him at it and Neil nearly killed him. They had him see a shrink. The shrink said that he should get a dishonorable discharge but no time in the brig. He came to my little apartment off campus. He was so angry about things he scared me.

"He'd always taken advantage of people before—I was able to see that then—and he got some kind of thrill out of stealing and fighting and conning people. But I thought that with everything he'd gone through—I thought maybe he'd want to straighten out for the first time in his life.

"And at first when he came to the commune he was really laid-back. Really cool in a way he'd never been before. I'd see him out back of the barn planting along with some of the others and I'd get tears in my eyes. I really believed that God had granted him another chance. Neil always laughed when I told him that I prayed a lot. But I didn't care. I kept right on praying for him. And everything was fine until he fell in love with Van. She was so beautiful I couldn't blame him. But by then Nicole and I were friends and she told me how Van used guys to hurt her father. She wanted to humiliate him by being a whore. I tried to tell him that but he just accused me of being jealous. I just couldn't deal with him anymore."

She was more silhouette than person perched there on the railing. I said, "But you knocked me out so he could escape."

"I was afraid for him. I was thinking maybe he really did kill Van. I didn't want him to go to prison."

"But then you couldn't take it anymore when he got Nicole pregnant."

She flipped her cigarette into the air, a blazing rocket ship against the moon-bright night. "Nicole is a kid. That's why I liked her right away. She's kind of innocent. We had lunch in the city park one day and she brought along a bunch of Archie comic books and talked about how Veronica reminded her of Van in a lot of ways. I laughed about that for a week. She was like this goofy little kid sister I never had. And when he got her pregnant—he couldn't at least have used a rubber?"

I stood up. "Don't tell me any more. We need to get you that lawyer first. I'll start calling as soon as I get home."

"You going to take me in yourself or have the cops come out here?"

"You got a preference?"

She came over and slid her arms around me. "I'm really scared." She seemed to fight her tears at first but then she was crying so hard her fear and sorrow came in great spasms.

We said very little on the drive back to town. There wasn't much point in talking, I guess.

22

'd gone to law school with David Brunner. He was now a prominent criminal defense attorney in Chicago. You can correctly assume he was a whole lot smarter than I'll ever be. I explained the case to him and told him that we could cover his fees. The largesse was coming from one Paul Mainwaring. As Marsha explained to me over the phone, Nicole was near a breakdown worrying about her friend Sarah. Mainwaring had saddled her and her sister with a sneering, duplicitous wife and an open marriage so he now saw that he needed to save his daughter. Marsha also told me that Paul and Eve had had two warring days of shouting at each other and that Eve had suddenly packed three suitcases and had taken a room at the Drake in Chicago.

Brunner was in the middle of a trial but promised he'd have one of his assistant attorneys on a train within two hours, which he did. John Silverman was in my office by late afternoon. I briefed him and then took him to the police station to meet Mike Potter and Cliffie. He and Potter got along in a reassuringly professional way. A way that was spoiled when Cliffie came in and began to pontificate about the case and warn John that "out-of-town lawyers" never did well in Black River Falls. He also reminded me several times that he said from the beginning Neil was the killer. Potter and Cliffie left us then to wait for somebody to escort us to a room where we could talk with Sarah. "I can't fucking believe that guy," Silverman said. Twice. A mild reaction compared to some when Cliffie was the subject.

The good Reverend Cartwright was presently housed on the fourth floor of the Protestant hospital, where he was making a fraudulent saga of being struck by lightning. He had been pronounced fine by the emergency doc and fine by his own doc, but the Rev insisted he was suffering from terrible but unspecified health problems that only hospital rest could cure. He bravely broadcast from his hospital bed, where he announced a "Fund Drive for the True Friends of Jesus." He said that God had told him he would recover at the same rate that money poured into church coffers. He never runs out of gimmicks, and damned if most of them don't work.

Four nights after taking Sarah to the police station, I got home late and weary. I'd been in court all afternoon and the central air there had worked only intermittently. Everybody in Court B was in a surly mood, me included. During lunch, assistant prosecutor, Hillary Fitzgerald, stopped on the step where I was eating my burger from the courthouse menu and said, "I feel sorry for your client, McCain. I've never seen Judge Hammond this nasty. Your guy is facing a DUI and I think Hammond is going to give him the chair." She had a winsome smile.

When I was coming up to the house, I saw that something was wrong. I hadn't been able to contact Wendy by phone. Now the lights were out and the house had a deserted look. Where had she gone?

Her car was in the garage. Had a friend picked her up?

I hurried to the back door and walked inside. We never locked up until we went to bed.

Refrigerator thrum. Air conditioner whoosh. All those inexplicable sounds of a house talking to itself.

Downstairs empty. Upstairs—

I went straight to our bedroom and there with the bloody sunset filling the window like a wound she lay in a tight fetal position in the center of the bed. Her blue walking shorts and white blouse were badly wrinkled, something she would ordinarily not have allowed.

The bedroom décor was all hers, of course. And it was very feminine, with a canopy bed, a doll collection, a dressing table, enough perfumes to enchant a sultan, and three stacks of fashion magazines from her high school years. I knew this because one night when she was depressed she sat in a chair in the living room with several very old issues, going through them with great interest. I asked her about them and she said, "That was the last time my life was simple. Back when I used to sit next to you in homeroom."

I knew she was aware of me because the sound of her breathing came sharper now. But she kept her eyes closed. When I saw the envelope on the hardwood floor I reached down to pick it up.

"Don't look at it." Her eyes were still closed; she hadn't moved.

But I did pick it up. I knew what it would be of course. Her mood told me that.

"We're going to Canada."

"No, we're not, Wendy."

Then she was not only sitting up, she was hurling herself off the bed and standing in front of me.

"Well, you're sure as hell not going to Nam, I'll tell you that. I lost my husband over there; I'm not going to lose you the same way."

"I have to go, Wendy. It's my duty. Other guard units have gone."

"Don't give me any patriotic bullshit. I don't want to hear it." I took it as significant that she wasn't crying. Her fury wouldn't allow for any softer expressions of pain.

I reached out for her but she jerked away. "Don't touch me. I can't believe you're just going to go along with this."

"What the hell choice do I have, Wendy?"

"Go to Canada. Or say you're a pacifist. Or say you're queer. Some goddamned thing. You're a lawyer, Sam. Start thinking like one."

She was doing me a kind of favor. By having to deal with her I didn't have to deal with my own feelings—fear and anger just like hers—that would be mine when I was alone.

"And think of your mother, Sam. How's she going to take this? She needs you just the same as I do."

I knew better than to touch her. "Listen, honey. Why don't you fix us a couple of drinks while I wash up? Then we can sit on the patio and talk this through a little more calmly."

"Don't give me your calmly bullshit, Sam. That's what you always say when you can't think of anything else." Then she waved me off. "This is making me so crazy. I'm like I was after my husband died." She looked crazy, too. Then, "I'll go make some drinks."

In the upstairs bathroom I washed up, and as I did I studied my face in the mirror. I knew what she meant about those old magazines. My face had been very different back then. If I survived the war it would change even more and probably not to my liking.

I'd been taking my time in the bathroom until I heard her weeping downstairs. Great harsh gushes that must have burned her throat.

I hurried up then. I needed to be with her for both our sakes.

THE END